"I'm pretty beat myself," Gwen said, a bit too brightly. "I think I'll head on to bed. Thank yo—"

Will interrupted her, knowing full well he wasn't going to let her retreat behind closed doors just yet. "There are a couple of things we still need to clear up."

"Really? What do you...?" She trailed off as he closed the slight distance between them, and she took two small steps backward—only to find her back against the foyer wall. Her eyes flashed as he took advantage of her position and moved to within inches of her body.

Reaching out, he captured the errant lock of hair that draped across her shoulder again. Twisting it around his finger, he played with the silky strand until her breathing became shallow.

"First, business and pleasure are two totally separate situations. I'm not one to confuse the two, and I'm surely not going to deny myself one just because I hired you to work. This—" he released her hair, only to move his hand to the elegant column of her neck, pleased to feel the pulse thumping wildly there "—has nothing to do with that."

Gwen's eyes widened as his other hand slid up her neck to cradle her jaw. She leaned in toward him, and he felt his own heartbeat accelerate.

"Second, Miss Behavior, I don't give a damn about what's appropriate."

kept for his
Pleasure

She's his mistress on demand!

Whether seduction takes place in his king-size bed, a five-star hotel, his office or beachside penthouse, these fabulously wealthy, charismatic and sexy men know how to keep a woman coming back for more! Commitment might not be high on his agenda—or even on it at all!

She's his mistress on demand—but when he wants her body *and* soul he will be demanding a whole lot more! Dare we say it…even marriage!

Don't miss any books in this exciting miniseries from Harlequin Presents®!

Kimberly Lang

THE MILLIONAIRE'S MISBEHAVING MISTRESS

kept for his
Pleasure

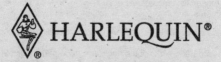

HARLEQUIN®

TORONTO • NEW YORK • LONDON
AMSTERDAM • PARIS • SYDNEY • HAMBURG
STOCKHOLM • ATHENS • TOKYO • MILAN • MADRID
PRAGUE • WARSAW • BUDAPEST • AUCKLAND

Recycling programs
for this product may
not exist in your area.

ISBN-13: 978-0-373-12866-2

THE MILLIONAIRE'S MISBEHAVING MISTRESS

First North American Publication 2009.

All about the author...
Kimberly Lang

KIMBERLY LANG hid romance novels behind her textbooks in junior high, and even a master's program in English couldn't break her obsession with dashing heroes and happily ever after. A ballet dancer turned English teacher, Kimberly married an electrical engineer and turned her life into an ongoing episode of *When Dilbert Met Frasier*. She and her Darling Geek live in beautiful north Alabama with their Amazing Child—who, unfortunately, shows an aptitude for sports.

Visit Kimberly at www.booksbykimberly.com for the latest news—and don't forget to say hi while you're there!

For the women who made all this possible.

Andrea Laurence, Marilyn Puett, Kira Sinclair and
Danniele Worsham—who are more than just my
playfriends and the sisters-of-my-heart, they are
also some of the smartest, most talented,
and infinitely patient women I've ever been
lucky enough to know.

Linda Winstead Jones, Linda Howard and
Beverly Barton—who let me learn at the
feet of the masters…I mean mavens.

Pamela Hearon—who broke me of a lot of
my bad habits in the nicest way possible.

And Bryony Green and Lucy Gilmour—
whose editorial brilliance is matched
only by their excellent taste.

CHAPTER ONE

"Evie is Bradley Harrison's daughter. I can't just lock her in the attic and pretend she doesn't exist!"

"You cannot continue to send her out in society as she is, either, William. She's an embarrassment to the family *and* the company."

Will Harrison poured another two fingers of Scotch and tipped the bottle in the direction of his late father's oldest friend and HarCorp's company attorney. So lunch at the Club yesterday hadn't gone as expected. It wasn't the end of the world.

Marcus Heatherton held out his glass for the refill. "Evangeline is a sweet girl, but Rachel let her run wild after your father died. You see the results. The child is a complete hoyden."

Now there's a word you don't hear every day. Hoyden. Much nicer sounding than "ill-mannered," "socially inept" or "tomboyish"—all of which had, unfortunately, been applied to his half sister.

The smile caused by Marcus's word choice faded. The image of a petit four flying out of Evie's wildly gesticulating hand and landing on the head of Mrs. Wellford's spoiled lapdog like a little hat flashed through his mind. That had been funny. The ensuing regurgitation of said petit four in Mrs. Wellford's lap after Shu-Shu swallowed it whole...well, that pretty much ended Evie's most recent foray into Dallas society on a distinctly low note.

At seventy, Marcus possessed old-fashioned ideas about proper upbringing for young ladies, but old-fashioned or not, he was right. Fifteen-year-old Evie had no manners, no social protocol and, as Marcus had been reminding Will for the last half-hour, *he* had to do something about it.

Or else the Harrison name would be gossip column fodder once again.

When his father announced his engagement to a company secretary half his age, everyone but him easily pegged Rachel for the gold digger she was. Bradley, though, either couldn't see or didn't care, and he smiled benignly in the background as Rachel ran circles around him, spending his money like it was going out of style and making him the laughingstock of the very society she'd worked so hard to infiltrate.

When Rachel tired of Dallas, Bradley officially retired and moved her and five-year-old Evie to the Caribbean, leaving Will in charge of the family company at the ripe old age of twenty-six.

And while Will dedicated the next ten years to running the company and expanding it into an international force, his father and Rachel frolicked on the beaches around St. Kitts and traveled the world, but made no attempt to prepare Evie for her place in Dallas society—or civilization in general, as far as Marcus was concerned.

Will hadn't heard much from Rachel in the last couple of years—after his father's death, she'd been little more than another issue for the accountant to deal with—but after the accident last month that had left her daughter an orphan, he'd found himself Evie's guardian.

So far, it hadn't been easy. Yesterday had just been the proverbial last straw for Marcus.

Will cleared his throat. "Mrs. Gray and her tutors…"

"Mrs. Gray is a housekeeper. She's kind to Evangeline and makes sure you both eat well and have clean clothes, but she is hardly the person to teach the child anything about etiquette.

Evangeline's tutors, even if they were qualified, need to focus on her studies so she'll be ready to start at Parkline Academy in the fall."

Marcus could be remarkably and frustratingly single-minded at times, but he'd been the one unwavering pillar of Will's life, completely dedicated to the company and the Harrison family. Evie's arrival had given the old man new focus, and for that, Will was grateful. His own love life and the need for a new generation of Harrisons had been under Marcus's microscope for far too long. At least he hadn't revisited the idea of Will marrying in order to give Evie a female role model. *Yet.* The night was still young, though, so he needed to think fast.

"William?"

"All right, I'll hire someone specifically to work with her on this—to teach her some manners and how to behave in polite society."

"You must do it *now*, William. People are already asking where Evangeline is and why you haven't introduced her to more of your father's friends or her own peer group. I've held everyone off for weeks now, claiming she needs more time to mourn her mother's passing."

"She does need time." His own mother had died when he was twelve; Will could relate to Evie's grief. At least he hadn't lost both parents so early in life. His father may have been distant, but he'd been around for the most part.

"Yes, but she has responsibilities that cannot be ignored now that she is back in the States."

"Responsibilities? She's fifteen, for God's sake. She doesn't *have* any responsibilities."

"Let me tell you this, William Harrison. Evangeline must be introduced into society and take her rightful place in it. Everyone is expecting to meet her at the Hospital Benefit."

With that pronouncement, Marcus sat back in his chair and swirled the Scotch in his glass, seemingly amused by Will's sputtering.

"The benefit? That's three weeks away."

"Then you'd better get busy finding someone, shouldn't you?"

Dear Miss Behavior,
I told my best friend I was hoping this guy we both like would ask me to go to a concert with him. She goes and buys tickets and then asks him to go with her! I'm so mad at her, but she says that if he'd liked me, then he wouldn't have agreed to go with her. Now she wants to borrow my leather jacket to wear on their date. She says it would be the "polite" thing to do since she loaned me a pair of boots the last time I had a date. I think she's the one being rude. Since we both love your column, I told her I'd let you decide. Do I have to loan her my jacket to go on a date with the guy I like?
Thnx.
Cinderella

Gwen reached for her coffee cup. Empty. She'd need at least another cup before she was awake enough to deal with teenage angst. She swiveled out of her chair and headed to the kitchen for a refill to fortify her before she waded in to the dangerous waters of adolescent controversy.

In the nine months she'd served as Miss Behavior, Teen Etiquette Expert on the TeenSpace Web site, she'd been embroiled in enough melodrama to write her own teenage soap opera. She'd signed on thinking she'd be answering simple questions like who asks whom to the prom or who pays for dinner. How wrong she was. The complexities of seating charts were child's play in comparison to the day-to-day drama of high school.

The coffee carafe was still half-full as she pulled it off the warmer and poured another extra-large cup. Her experience with teenage dramatics had been vicarious at best. She'd been the "good" daughter—except that one time—leaving her sister Sarah to reap Mother's wrath over her outlandish behavior. Funny how now, after all these years, she was still standing on the outskirts of the fray and trying to mediate the peace.

A yowl was Gwen's only warning as Letitia jumped from behind the pie safe to attack the ears of Gwen's bunny slippers, only to land claws first on her ankle instead. Coffee sluiced over her hand as she jumped, splattering to the floor around the black and white cat. Letitia hissed at the coffee puddles, took one last swipe at the slippers and bolted out of the kitchen.

"You're going to get burned doing that, you silly cat." Or declawed. This was a new trick from the previously laid-back Letitia. A gift from her sister, the new slippers with their oversize ears had pushed the cat over the edge. After five days of this, her ankles looked like she'd been attacked by a ravenous horde of three-inch vampires. The slippers were comfortable, not to mention cute, but not worth the constant battle. She left the slippers in the kitchen for Letitia to attack at her leisure and went back to her computer.

Stifling the urge to start with *"With friends like that, who needs enemies,"* Gwen typed out her response for Cinderella and posted all five of today's questions and answers to the site before logging out of her Miss Behavior account and turning her attention to the mail on her desk. Miss Behavior had been an instant Internet success, tripling the hits to TeenSpace in the last six months, and her real-life consulting business was benefiting from the popularity of the column. As much as she hated it sometimes, practically every debutante in Dallas had her on speed dial.

In addition to bills and a few checks her bank account desperately needed, the morning's snail mail brought yet another plaque of thanks from the Victorian Guild for her work with the current debutante class. She'd *earned* a plaque this year; that group of debs had been the worst yet. Just getting them to spit out their gum and turn off their cell phones had taken most of her patience.

She scanned her office, debating where she had room for it. Wall space was at a premium as debutante class photos, thank-you plaques and other memorabilia competed for a place. There was space over her certificates from some of the best protocol schools in the country, but she really didn't want anything relating to her current work next to them.

She sighed. If her classmates could see her now. Those certificates—many awarded with honors as the top student in her class—hung next to her degree from George Washington, all of which needed dusting. She was trained to work with politicians, heads of state and corporate bigwigs; instead, she spent her time with debutantes and cotillion clubs.

One day, she'd be able to quit teaching spoiled, rich teenagers to eat without their elbows on the table and go back to working with grown-ups in serious business.

Please, God.

For now, though, the teenagers of Texas were paying her rent. She pulled her file on the group of Junior League members who would be taking their daughters to D.C. next month. Teenage girls meeting senators was at least *one* step closer to getting back on track. She should be counting her blessings.

The three short rings of her business line caught her attention. She sat up straight, smiled and answered before the second set of rings finished.

"Good morning. Everyday Etiquette. This is Gwen Sawyer speaking."

"Miss Sawyer, this is Nancy Tucker calling from William Harrison's office at HarCorp International." The voice was cool, smooth and undeniably professional.

Gwen's heart beat double-time at the woman's words. She'd been trying to get her foot in the door at HarCorp for *months*. That dragon in Human Resources seemed so hellbent on ignoring her proposals, she'd almost given up. A squeal of glee wanted to escape, but she cleared her throat and concentrated on sounding just as professional as Ms. Tucker.

"Yes, Ms. Tucker, how may I help you?"

"Mr. Harrison would like to meet with you to discuss contracting your services. He realizes it's very short notice, but he could meet with you this afternoon at two, if you are available."

Adrenaline rushed through her system, and she began pulling files of proposals from her desk drawer. *Available?* She'd cancel a funeral to be there. Forget the HR dragon; the boss himself wanted to see her. "Two o'clock would be fine."

"Wonderful. I'll let the receptionist know to expect you." The carefully modulated tones didn't change.

"Thank you. I'll see you then." Only when the phone was securely in its cradle did Gwen release the squeal choking her.

This was it. Her days in debutante hell were finally over. After five long years of penance, she'd finally get the chance to restart her career. Ms. Tucker hadn't mentioned *what* kind of service HarCorp was looking for, but Gwen didn't care. If Will Harrison wanted to talk to her, it would have to be something important. Hadn't she seen an article in the paper not long ago that HarCorp was moving into the Asian market? Had someone passed along her proposals to the boss himself?

Talk about dream come true time… The Junior League file went back into the drawer, and she pulled out her folder on HarCorp and the ignored-until-now proposals. She didn't have much time to prepare, but deep down, she knew one thing.

This meeting was going to change her life.

Gwen checked her watch. One-fifty. Perfect. She'd killed the last five minutes in the ladies' room on HarCorp's fourteenth floor, not wanting to arrive *too* early. One last critical look in the mirror confirmed that she presented the best image possible. The wind in the parking lot had teased a few wispy tendrils of hair out of the severe French twist she'd forced her hair into earlier, but thankfully, the damage wasn't too drastic.

She powdered the freckles on her nose one last time and hoped the nervous flush on her cheeks would fade. Applying one last sweep of gloss across her lips, she studied the image in the mirror carefully. She wouldn't be winning any beauty pageants, but she looked responsible and mature—just like a protocol consultant should.

Camel-brown suit. Peach silk shirt. Closed-toe shoes with coordinating briefcase. Gramma Jane's pearls for luck. Gwen closed her eyes and inhaled deeply, willing herself to project cool, collected, *confident* professionalism.

Even if she was quivering so badly inside she thought she might be ill.

At one fifty-five, she opened the glass doors of the executive offices and presented herself to the receptionist.

"I'm Gwen Sawyer. I have a two o'clock appointment with Mr. Harrison."

The reception desk resembled the cockpit of the space shuttle: blinking buttons, keyboards and computer screens all within easy reach of the occupant. The nameplate on the desk identified the occupant as Jewel Madison, a detail Gwen noted so it could be added to the HarCorp file later. The Ms. Tucker she'd spoken to earlier must be Mr. Harrison's personal secretary.

Jewel consulted a screen. "Mr. Harrison has been held up in a meeting and is running a few minutes behind. He sends his apologies. You can have a seat over there." She waved in the direction of a seating area. "Would you like a cup of coffee while you wait?"

Coffee was the last thing her roiling stomach needed. As she declined, something on the desk beeped and Jewel's attention shifted. Dismissed, Gwen went to wait. A leather couch nicer than the ones in most people's homes looked too squishy to get up from gracefully, so she chose the less comfortable, but much more dignified wing chair instead. Copies of the HarCorp Annual Report covered the small coffee table and for lack of something else to do, Gwen picked one up and flipped through it absently as she mentally rehearsed her pitch one last time.

As a "few minutes" turned into twenty, then thirty, her irritation level rose steadily. At two thirty-five, a forty-something dark-haired woman in a lime-green suit turned the corner and introduced herself as the Nancy Tucker of that morning's phone call.

"So sorry you had to wait. Mr. Harrison can see you now."

About damn time, Gwen thought before she checked herself. *Breathe.* Don't get irritated. This is too important to get all twitchy about punctuality issues.

Nancy was all business. She led Gwen down the hallway in silence, no small talk at all, and delivered her to William Harrison's office door. After a quick knock, she opened it, ushering Gwen in ahead of her.

A stunning view of the Dallas skyline greeted her, but the occupant of the office did not. Without breaking his conversation with whomever was on the phone, he waved her in and indicated he'd be with her in just a minute.

Nancy guided her to one of the chairs facing the massive desk, then slipped silently out the door. Gwen set her briefcase on the floor, crossed one foot behind the other, folded her hands in her lap and waited.

Lesson number one: Don't talk on the phone while there's a flesh and blood person in front of you. Taking a deep breath, she kept her frustration to herself. He was a busy man, and he'd at least acknowledged her presence. So she sat quietly, but uncomfortably, as the conversation continued. Gwen tried to keep her gaze on the view of the city as it would be rude to stare at Will Harrison.

And she knew for certain that it *was* Will Harrison. She'd seen his picture in the papers enough to recognize him. While she might not run in the same circles of society as he, her clients certainly did, and as one of Dallas's Most Eligible Bachelors, many of her debs and their mammas were quite obsessed with him.

She could easily see why they were swooning. If she weren't so irritated, she might feel a teeny-tiny swoon coming on herself. None of his pictures did him justice. In person, he didn't look at all like a buttoned-up and stuffy Fortune 500 CEO. His collar and cuffs were both *un*buttoned in fact, his tie pulled loose at the knot and his sleeves rolled up over his forearms. His dark hair hung a little longer than most executives', and the tan on his face said he didn't spend all of his time in the boardroom. Gwen could easily picture him as the outdoorsy type, and the broad shoulders and strong arms indicated it was something far more active than executive golfing. Maybe he was one of those weekend cowboys? The office lacked any Western-themed decor, so that didn't help. She tried to casually scan his office for clues to his hobbies, telling herself it was strictly for business purposes...

A deep, rumbling chuckle jerked her attention back to the man behind the desk. This time, he caught her eye and smiled. It was the smile that nearly did her in. The man had a dimple, for God's sake, and the total effect would give any live woman a pulse spike.

And, if her pulse was any indication, she was very much alive at the moment. *Mercy.* Most Eligible, indeed. She stifled the urge to fan herself as the room grew a little too warm.

He was around the desk and extending his hand to her before she even realized he'd hung up the phone. "Sorry to keep you waiting, Miss Sawyer. Will Harrison."

Up close, the man was even more devastating to the senses. At this distance, Gwen could see that Will's eyes were hazel—not the murky hazel of her own, but a clear, perfect hazel. The hand he offered was strong and warm and sent a little tingle of electricity up her arm as she touched him. That swoon seemed more and more likely with each passing minute.

Focus, Gwen. She gave herself a mental shake. *You're not a groupie here to drool over the man. Pull it together because it's showtime.* "Not a problem." She opened her briefcase and pulled out several of her HarCorp folders. "Everyday Etiquette has a reputation—"

Will returned to his chair on the other side of the desk. "Nancy assures me you are the best at what you do, so I have no doubts you will be successful with Evie. However, we're on a deadline here, and I need to know you can work quickly. And, of course, your discretion is essential."

Irritation at being interrupted midsentence was tempered by the compliment that she was the best. She *was*, darn it; it was about time somebody took note. But how did Nancy know? And who was Evie? Discretion? What kind of training did HarCorp need?

"The Hospital Benefit is less than three weeks away. It's Evie's 'launch,' so to speak."

Confusion reigned. She knew exactly when the Med Ball was—it had been a major topic in one of her classes last week. But what did HarCorp have to do other than write a check? She cleared her throat, berating herself for not getting more details from Nancy that morning on the phone. "Mr. Harrison, Ms. Tucker didn't provide any specific information about what kind of services HarCorp needed, so I'm afraid I'm a bit at a loss as to what you are talking about."

Those black eyebrows shot up in surprise, but his computer pinged, and his attention moved to the screen. "Damn." His fingers flew across the keyboard before responding. "Evie is my sister—my half sister, actually."

Ah, the elusive Evangeline she'd read about. The society columns were buzzing with speculation… *Oh, no.* A bad feeling crept up her spine.

"She's living with me now, and her manners are atrocious. I need you to teach her how to be a lady. That is what you do, correct?"

Please let me be wrong. Please. "You need social training for your sister?"

"Table manners. Polite conversation. How to behave at a

party." Another ping from the computer, and his eyes went immediately to the screen. "And she'll need help with her wardrobe as well."

Damn. Her heart sank as what was left of her hopes evaporated. HarCorp didn't need her—another spoiled debutante did. Just to be sure, she asked, "And how old is Evie?"

"Fifteen."

Gwen tried to keep her disappointment out of her voice. "Fifteen's a bit young for debutante training, don't you think? Surely you have a few more years before…"

That got his full attention. She trailed off as he pinned her with those hazel eyes, and his voice took on a sharp edge. "She's not a debutante. She's an heiress and a Harrison." He said "Harrison" like it was a synonym for "royalty." "Sadly, my father and stepmother didn't see to it that Evie learn how to behave properly in public before they died. Evie needs someone to teach her, and she needs to know enough not to embarrass herself or the family at the Hospital Benefit. It's pretty straightforward."

This time, it was the phone on his desk that beeped, drawing his attention away again with only an offhanded "excuse me" as he answered it. Irritation bloomed again before she could help it. She dug her nails into her palm and bit her tongue. Good manners meant she couldn't call him on his rudeness—and busy man or not, he was starting to really fray her Miss Behavior nerves.

Good manners also meant she shouldn't eavesdrop on his conversation, and she needed a moment to think and regroup anyway.

She shouldn't be upset that he wanted her to do social training—it was, after all, her primary source of income at the moment, and she was very good at it. Her pride was just a bit bruised because she'd come in with such high hopes for something else. She should agree to work with his sister…maybe some of the lessons would rub off on him.

That thought kindled her hopes again. Maybe, just maybe, *this* was the way into HarCorp. The back way in, granted, but she'd take what she could get. She'd work with the sister and hope that the brother would be so impressed he'd listen to her proposals for business training…

"Well, Miss Sawyer, what do you think?" Will's attention was back on her, and she straightened her spine. Even with her irritation, she had to be impressed with how he could jump from one task to another and not lose track of either. Will steepled his fingers as he leaned back in his chair, one eyebrow raised in question.

"I'd be glad to work with your sister, Mr. Harrison, but three weeks is not a lot of time…"

"Exactly. You'll need every spare minute with Evie." He reached for a pen and scribbled something on a piece of paper before rounding the desk once again. This time, though, he leaned his hips back against it as he handed her the paper.

Dragging her thoughts from the long legs stretched out so close to her, she blinked and tried to focus on the bold scrawl.

An address in the elite Turtle Creek neighborhood.

"I've told the housekeeper, Mrs. Gray, to prepare the guest room. You can move your things in tonight and start with Evie tomorrow."

Heat rushed to her cheeks at the thought, and she struggled to find words. "M-m-move in? Are you—I mean, that's not—" She took a deep breath to calm the unprofessional stuttering caused by his presumptuous statement. "I have a business to run—other clients and responsibilities." *And the papers would have a field day.*

"Evie spends several hours a day with her tutors catching up on schoolwork. That would give you some time to take care of your other responsibilities. I'm quite willing to pay you for the inconvenience."

She had to call on years of training not to react at the outrageous figure he mentioned. He *was* serious about this.

"And, as I said earlier, your discretion is essential."

Discretion? For that amount of money he could silence *Dallas Lifestyles*'s gossip columnist.

She was younger than he'd expected. Prettier, too, in a whole-some girl-next-door kind of way. She lacked that brittle edge that often came with sophistication—a nice contrast from the women he was used to.

He'd been expecting a plump, gray-haired, grandmotherly type—or, at the very least, a Mary Poppins—if for no other reason he felt anyone calling herself an expert on anything should at least look old enough to drink. Miss Gwen Sawyer was neither plump nor grandmotherly and probably got carded on a regular basis. At the same time, she projected a kind of cool elegance that fascinated him and that Evie would benefit from learning.

She acted completely calm and professional, but he knew she wasn't as detached as she looked. While Miss Sawyer was capable of keeping a good poker face, she couldn't control those wide hazel eyes of hers that expressed each and every feeling the moment she had it. And she'd experienced several throughout their interview. Calculation, shock, confusion—she'd worked through them all. At least once, he'd even seen irritation there, but he wasn't sure why. But something *had* thrown Gwen off her game very early on in the meeting, and it had taken a few minutes for her to regroup. He still hadn't figured out what that had been about, either.

He expected the money to throw her off-guard. It was much more than such services could possibly cost, but it would assure she'd give Evie her full attention and keep her mouth closed to Tish Cotter-Hulme, the local society gossip columnist.

Gwen regained her balance much more quickly this time, covering her discomfort with cool politeness. Nice trick. Hopefully she could teach it to Evie.

"I couldn't possibly move into your home."

"Are you married?" He glanced down to where her fingers laced together in her lap. The white knuckles gave away her agitation as clearly as her eyes did, but from his position, he couldn't see if she wore a ring or not.

"Excuse me?" Her eyebrows flew toward her hairline in shock, and a flush stained her cheeks.

"Are you married? Do you have children or something?" Gwen took a deep breath before answering, and he realized he was a little *too* interested in her response.

"No, but—"

"Good." He let out the breath he'd been holding. "I understand the request is a bit odd—" Gwen gave him a wonderful *"you think?"* look that would have been funny in a different situation, so he forged ahead before she could mount a stronger rejection of his offer. "But Evie's still recovering from her mother's death. She's a little fragile at times and having a hard time adjusting. She needs someone who can give her undivided attention. It would be easier on her to have you there full-time."

He could see Gwen softening.

She played with the pearls at her neck, calling his attention to the flush rising from the collar of her blouse. "I guess I could—"

"Excellent."

Gwen took a deep breath, and her hand fell back to her lap. When she spoke, that cool professionalism was back. In a way he was disappointed; a slightly rattled Gwen was much more interesting.

"I'll prepare a contract and fax it to your secretary this afternoon."

"And I have a nondisclosure agreement that will require your signature as well. I don't want Evie embarrassed or details of my private life shared with the papers."

"Of course. I understand completely." She stood, and he rose to his feet. Although he topped her by a good seven inches, she pushed her shoulders back and looked him squarely in the eye for the first time since he'd rattled her with his unorthodox proposal. "I'll gather my things and be at your home tonight around six-thirty or so. Will that be acceptable?"

Her words caused a smile. He didn't know much about etiquette, but Miss Sawyer would make one hell of an executive if she put her mind to it. He was looking forward to seeing her in action with Evie.

"That'll be fine. I'll tell Mrs. Gray to serve dinner around seven."

She offered her hand. "I'll see you then. It was nice meeting you, Mr. Harrison."

"Call me Will."

"And I'm Gwen. I'll see you tonight."

With another of those cool, polite smiles, Gwen Sawyer showed herself to the door, allowing him the opportunity to observe what he'd missed earlier by being on the phone when she arrived. Long legs. Nice curves almost camouflaged by a conservative suit. A graceful and unhurried walk.

Hopefully Evie would take to her.

He couldn't help but think back to the evening two nights ago. After Marcus left, he'd found Evie on the stairs, tears glistening in the corners of her eyes. Evie took after Rachel with her auburn hair and high cheekbones, but she had her father's—*their* father's—eyes. Unsure how to handle a teary teenager, he'd joined her on the steps but said nothing.

Evie broke the silence first. "I'm sorry I'm such an embarrassment to you."

She must have overhead Marcus's comments. "You're not an embarrassment. You just don't know what it's like here." He patted her shoulder, feeling awkward as he did. He was still new to this big brother thing.

"I'm willing to learn, Will. I promise I'll work really hard." She swallowed hard as the tears overflowed. "Please don't send me away."

"Away?"

"To boarding school. I heard Uncle Marcus mention it last week. I don't want to go. Please, Will."

Guilt at even considering Marcus's suggestion nagged at him. "You're not going to boarding school. You're a Harrison, and this is where you belong."

Evie's tear-streaked face split into a wide grin as she launched herself into his arms.

Parenting a teenager still had him confused, but he'd bridged a gap that night with Evie. He barely knew her—partly due to the difference in their ages and partly because he'd simply been too busy to concern himself with a child several thousand miles away. But they were getting to know each other now and coming to an agreeable living arrangement.

He was getting the hang of this after all. With the addition of Gwen Sawyer to the team, his life could start working itself back to normal.

And, just to be sure, he'd be home for Gwen's arrival tonight.

CHAPTER TWO

"You *are* kidding me, right? *The* Will Harrison hired you? I didn't even know he had a sister."

"That's because you don't read the society section closely enough. And don't sound so surprised. As I've been reminded more than once recently, social training *is* what I do for a living." Gwen balanced the phone on her shoulder as she loaded her laptop into its case.

Sarah went into Sister Support Mode. "Temporarily, Gwennie, temporarily. Even if the kid eats with her feet, you'll turn her into Jackie O in no time. Then, big brother will *have* to listen to what you can do for his company."

"I can hope." Gwen consulted her list. Laptop. Dinner kit. Tea kit. Etiquette books for her new client. Her suitcase. Check, check, check and check.

The increase in background noise meant her sister was no longer alone. Hastily she added, "Listen, you can't tell anyone about this. 'My discretion is essential,' remember?"

"Ich verstehe." Sarah switched to German, a tactic they'd used for years when they didn't want others to understand their conversation. "Is he as handsome as his pictures?"

Better than his pictures. Yummy, actually. "Oh, grow up, Sarah."

"He's Dallas's Most Eligible Bachelor, you know."

"One of them, at least," she hedged.

"Seriously, what's he like?"

"Busy. A bit brusque. In need of one of my refresher classes." Gwen grabbed her address book and current client files and added them to the growing pile. Will Harrison might be the biggest client she'd signed on, but she still had to take care of the others.

"Well, maybe your lessons with his sister will rub off on him."

Gwen responded with an unladylike, but noncommittal "humph" as she dragged her suitcase down the hallway. "One more thing. Can you look after Letitia for a while?"

"Sure, Gwennie. Why?"

"This is where *your* discretion comes in. I'm going to be living with the Harrisons for the next couple of weeks." Gwen held the phone away from her ear in expectation of her sister's reaction.

"You're *what?*" Even with the phone several inches away, she clearly heard every one of the dozen rapid-fire questions delivered at the top of her sister's voice.

"Calm down. Good Lord, you sound exactly like Mother when you do that."

"That's uncalled for."

"Well, if the shoe fits…"

"You do understand that if that columnist from *Dallas Lifestyles* gets wind of this, she'll have a field day with you."

"There's nothing nefarious going on. I'm moving into the guest bedroom so I'll have total access to Evie. If *my* over-developed sense of propriety can handle it, so can yours." She consulted her list one last time. Surely she had everything she needed. It wasn't like she was going to Siberia or anything. "Since when do you care what people think anyway?"

Sarah sighed. "That's my point. I don't, but *you* need to. Let me remind you that the majority of your clientele is hugely conservative. Proper debutante trainers don't live with men they aren't related to."

"I know, I know. This is why you need to keep your mouth shut. Should anyone find out—"

"And you know they will, Gwennie. Will Harrison is one of that Hulme woman's favorite subjects for her column. Do you honestly think you can move in to his house and no one will notice?"

It was Gwen's turn to sigh. "I'll cross that bridge when I get to it. This is a business arrangement, nothing more. No one would question it if he'd hired a live-in housekeeper. This isn't any different."

"I'd keep practicing that statement, if I were you. I think you're going to need it."

"There's no need to sound so dire. It's not like there's paparazzi staking out his building or anything. If I just lie low and not call attention to myself, this should stay under the radar."

"Good luck with that." Gwen could almost hear Sarah's eyes rolling with the sarcasm.

"Jeez, thanks for the vote of support."

"You have my support—you know that. I also know how hard you've worked to build something here, and I'd hate for you to lose ground again."

"I know. But I just get the feeling this is the right thing to do. That it's my chance. I've got to try. If not, I'm afraid I'm going to spend another five years playing with place settings."

"Then I'll keep my fingers and toes crossed for you."

"Thank you. Now can you come get Letitia and keep her until I'm finished with Evie?"

"Of course."

"And speaking of Evie, can I bring her in to see you this week? Seems she's going to need a wardrobe."

She heard the clicks from the keyboard that meant Sarah was checking her schedule. "I'm free Friday afternoon," she finally said. "Will that work? Monday morning would be okay, too. Just let me know."

"Thanks. I'm already running late so I really have to go. I'll have my cell if you need me. And remember, *discretion*."

"Genau." Sarah switched back to English. "Call me tomorrow. I want to hear all the juicy details."

"Good*bye*." *There will be no juicy details this time.*

The brief foray into German reminded Gwen to go back to her office for her Japanese dictionary and software. If she wanted to promote herself as an expert in Asian relations, she needed to get her fluency back in Japanese. Which meant she was dependent on software for the time being. Hopefully Evie *didn't* eat with her feet and she'd have some time to practice...

As she loaded her car, she questioned her sanity one last time. If all went well, this could change everything for her. If she could just get HarCorp as a satisfied customer, every company in Dallas would be lining up for her services. Heck, HarCorp could open doors for her all over Texas.

But if Evie wasn't ready in time...she could kiss most of her clientele goodbye. Sarah wasn't wrong about her business suffering if the gossip columns decided to portray her as some kind of immoral floozy. But the true Worst Case Scenario was if she didn't produce the results Will Harrison expected. Unhappy Harrisons spelled certain doom for her entire business— including the debs. No one would hire her for anything if the Harrisons blacklisted her. The Dallas elite were a close-knit group. Alienating one meant alienating them all.

This was make or break time.

Nothing like a little pressure to keep a girl on her toes. She shifted into Drive and tried to think positively.

On a map, Will Harrison's high-rise building might be only four miles from her funky M Street cottage, but in terms of wealth, Gwen felt like she'd traveled to the moon.

She stopped under the porte cochere where a doorman met her at her car and introduced himself as Michael. She identified herself, half expecting to be told to move her simple Honda to a less-affluent area.

"Miss Sawyer, of course. Mr. Harrison said to expect you. Let me help you with your things, and Ricky will take your car to the garage."

The helpful doorman made easy conversation as he gathered her gear from the trunk and escorted her to the elevator. "The Harrisons are in Penthouse A."

Of course they are. Where else would they live? Michael pushed the button marked P, and she gasped as the elevator sped to the top floor in seconds and deposited them almost directly in front of the door marked A.

"I cannot believe I'm doing this," she muttered.

"Excuse me?" Michael asked from behind her.

"Oh, nothing." With one last mental slap to the forehead, she rang the bell.

She heard a voice shout "I'll get it!" before the door was thrown open by a teenage girl she had to assume was Evie.

The girl's dark red hair was braided into cornrows tipped with colorful beads that swung dangerously as she turned to shout, "Will, she's here!" She waved Gwen in and smiled at Michael as he returned to the elevator.

Evie's casual air and easy manner contrasted sharply with the cool marble elegance of the foyer. Tall and thin in the way only teenagers can be, she wore faded blue jeans frayed at the hems and a gauzy white peasant shirt. While she was barefoot and fresh-faced now, Evie would be a raving beauty once she matured out of the gangly awkwardness of adolescence. Gwen remembered the picture of Bradley Harrison that hung in the HarCorp lobby; Evie must have inherited her amazing bone structure from her mother. Neither she nor Will favored Bradley Harrison at all, except for their eyes.

Just as she thought his name, Will appeared from a room farther down the hall. Her breath caught in her chest. The suit and tie were gone, replaced by a pair of faded jeans and a snug blue T-shirt that clearly outlined the shoulders she'd admired earlier in his office. Tanned biceps flexed as he helped Gwen bring her suitcase in.

He, too, was barefoot, and she felt ridiculously out-of-place: overdressed in her suit and sensible shoes and totally dumpy standing next to such perfect specimens of beauty.

"Gwen, this is my sister, Evangeline. Evie, this is Miss Sawyer."

Pulling herself together, Gwen offered her hand to Evie. "I'm very pleased to meet you, Evangeline. May I call you Evie as well?"

"Ohmigod, you really are Miss Behavior, aren't you?"

Gwen ignored Will's uplifted eyebrows. "Yes, I am. I take it you read my column?"

Evie bounced on the balls of her feet. "Every single day since Mrs. Gray told me I had to learn some manners. Plus all the archive stuff, too. I've learned so much already. I can't believe Will got *you* as my teacher! Cool!"

"Then let's try this again." Gwen offered her hand to Evie a second time. "It's nice to meet you, Evangeline."

Evie took the hint and with a sideways glance at Will tried again. "It's nice to meet you too, Miss Sawyer. Please call me Evie." Evie shook her hand, but it was a timid handshake. They'd work on that tomorrow.

"Since we're going to be working closely together, why don't you call me Gwen?"

Evie grinned, and Gwen knew she had a winner on her hands.

"Evie, take Gwen's things to her room." Evie disappeared around a corner, dragging Gwen's suitcase behind her, and Will lifted an eyebrow at her. "Miss Behavior?"

"On the TeenSpace site. Kind of like Miss Manners." He finally guided her out of the foyer and into a living area with another spectacular view of Dallas. The man must really like looking out over the skyline. "That's why Evie knew what I was talking about there in the hallway. We went over introductions just last week on the site."

He nodded and changed the subject abruptly. "Mrs. Gray will have dinner ready in just a minute or two. Would you like a drink?"

Desperately. But she shook her head and declined. She needed her A-game tonight, and a drink wouldn't help. Perching carefully in the wing chair opposite his, she tried to make small talk. It wasn't easy.

Will picked up his glass from the coffee table and swirled the amber liquid. Scotch? Bourbon? she wondered briefly, then lost her train of thought as he leaned back in the chair and propped his feet on the edge of the coffee table. They were large and tanned, and for reasons she couldn't begin to explore, oddly fascinating to her.

"Gwen?"

She snapped back to the conversation and felt the guilty flush creep up her neck. She'd been staring at his *feet,* for goodness sake. What on earth was wrong with her?

She smiled an apology.

"You can get settled in after dinner. Please make yourself at home. If you need anything, just let Mrs. Gray know."

"Thank you."

"Now, let's talk about Evie."

Another complete turnaround. Will got bonus points for remembering the small pleasantries, but he remained focused on why she was here.

"What about me?" Evie came into the room and flopped on the sofa.

"I want to hear how Gwen's going to miraculously turn you into a lady before the Hospital Benefit. *You* should be sitting up straight and paying attention."

Evie straightened up and both Harrison siblings looked at her expectantly.

Good God. What have I gotten myself into? "Well…"

Mrs. Gray chose that moment to call them to dinner and Gwen sent up a word of thanks. This was the strangest situation of her career, and she wasn't sure how to proceed. Dinner would make this much easier.

How wrong she was. Evie chattered like a magpie, covering every topic that crossed her mind, from the TeenSpace site and Gwen's column to how much she disliked the food in America. Will said little, occasionally commenting on Evie's monologue when she paused for a breath, and when his BlackBerry beeped in the next room, he went to get it and brought it back to the table with him.

Gwen watched it all in a state of mild shock.

"So, how do you become a manners expert, Gwen? Is there like a school someplace or something?" Evie perched her chin on her fist and gave Gwen her full attention for the first time during the meal. Will even looked up from his Black-Berry to hear her answer.

Well, at least it was some progress. "There are several schools, actually. I have a B.A. in International Affairs, and I've attended protocol schools on both coasts. But my family was in the Foreign Service, so I've spent my entire life—"

"Really? Cool! Where did you live?" Evie spoke in a series of exclamation points, which wouldn't be too bad if she would stop interrupting.

"D.C., Germany, England, Japan. Asian culture is a special interest of mine." While she had Will's attention, Gwen debated adding more to that statement in hopes he'd make the connection to what she could do for HarCorp's expansion plans. The opportunity was lost almost immediately, though, as Evie sped on to the next topic of what was beginning to feel like an inquisition.

"Did you have to go to special classes and stuff so you wouldn't embarrass your parents?"

"Um, sometimes. My mother's a fiend for proper manners, and she taught me most of what I needed to know. Otherwise, I wouldn't have been allowed in public." She punctuated the statement with a grin, but Evie stiffened and glanced at Will.

Okay, that may have been a sore spot for *her,* but she'd meant the statement to be funny. With the slight tightening of Will's jaw as well, she realized her attempt at humor had fallen flat. The light mood turned tense. So, it seemed *that* was a touchy subject in the Harrison household as well. She hurried on to cover the awkward moment. "But a lot can be learned from books, so I brought you some reading material."

Evie rolled her eyes. "More homework."

Will pushed his chair back from the table and stood. "You'll have to excuse me, ladies. I have a conference call in ten minutes. I'll leave you two to get to know each other." A second later, he was gone.

Evie merely nodded and went back to her dinner. Gwen, however, felt her jaw hit the table before she could stop it. Jeez-Louise. A certain amount of laxity was allowed at family meals, but this was ridiculous. She chose her words carefully. "Is this a normal occurrence?"

Evie poked at her peas. "Not really."

Gwen felt her shoulders sag. "Oh, good."

Continuing to push her peas around aimlessly, Evie didn't seem to notice Gwen's relief. "Will normally eats in his office if he's home. Sometimes we'll watch a movie or something while we eat." She looked around the dining room with interest. "You know, I think this is the first time I've eaten in here."

Gwen choked, then swallowed her lecture on the importance of family meals taken at the table. Her own parents had been such sticklers for family meals, partly due to Mother's abhorrence of the mere *idea* of a TV tray. One of the first things she did when she moved out on her own was to eat dinner in the living room. She'd felt so rebellious, she nearly had to call home to brag about her indiscretion.

Evie sat up straight in her chair, drawing Gwen's attention back to the situation at hand. "How am I doing? Am I hopeless?"

The earnest, expectant look on her face was so different from the usual teenagers that suffered through her classes, and

Gwen's heart clenched at Evie's need to please. "You're not hopeless at all, just a little rough around the edges. Would you like to start your lessons tonight?"

Evie's eager nod would have been almost comical if Gwen hadn't seen that need exposed earlier. "Then sit up straight, feet on the floor…"

"It's taken care of, Marcus. Evie's lessons start today." The old man could be such a nag.

"Who did you hire? Did you check her references?"

Will hadn't; that's what he paid his secretary for. But Marcus didn't need to know that. "Gwen Sawyer came highly recommended. She does debutante training."

Nancy came in with his third cup of coffee and an armload of reports, giving him an excuse to cut the conversation short without too much guilt. "Unless you have some company business to discuss…"

"No, no. Get back to work. I'll be by Thursday evening to meet this Miss Sawyer."

That was the problem with working with people who'd known you all your life, Will thought as he hung up the phone and turned to the stack of reports Nancy left on his desk. *They never believe you're actually an adult.* He was perfectly capable of hiring a tutor for his sister without Marcus's oversight.

Evie was certainly thrilled with Gwen. He'd seen her briefly this morning, and she'd chattered on in her usual nonstop fashion about all Gwen had taught her after he'd left the table. And she'd thanked him again for hiring the one and only Miss Behavior.

Evie's excitement was the reason he was currently surfing TeenSpace instead of concentrating on the reports from Tokyo littering his desk. Well, it was part of the reason. He had to admit he was a bit interested in Gwen Sawyer as well. Too bad he had to leave the table last night for that conference call—he'd been enjoying himself.

Telling himself it was his responsibility as Evie's guardian to check up on Gwen, he'd headed to the Web site Gwen mentioned the night before. TeenSpace was a headache-inducing riot of color and graphics about TV stars and bands he'd never heard of. In the top right-hand corner of the home page he found the link he was looking for. The "Miss Behavior" page loaded and Gwen's picture smiled at him over the phrase "More Than Forks and Tea Cups…Etiquette for the Twenty-First Century."

"Etiquette" seemed a pretty broad term for what Gwen was dispensing in her column. Drama and angst outnumbered true etiquette five to one. Gwen was certainly trying, though. In addition to letters from her readers, she had column after column of basic behavior skills. He had to give Gwen credit; she seemed to give sound advice that her readers accepted at face value, and she was extremely, well, *polite* about everything. Any reservations he might have been entertaining evaporated. Gwen was definitely the right choice for Evie. Out of curiosity, he typed "Miss Behavior" into Google. An article from the *Tribune* popped up first.

"She's Not Your Mother's Miss Manners"
Miss Behavior, the new etiquette expert on the Dallas-based TeenSpace Web site, has taken more than Dallas by storm. Hits to the teen-centered site have tripled since she came on board nine months ago, and she gets more e-mail from the site than any other columnist. Part Miss Manners, part Dear Abby, her answers to teens' modern-day etiquette dilemmas are succinct, sassy and spot-on. In real life, Miss Behavior is Gwen Sawyer, a Dallas etiquette consultant favored by debutantes…

Nancy buzzed the intercom, interrupting his reading.
"Mr. Harrison, Miss Sawyer is on line one."
Already? Had Evie pushed her over the edge in less than twenty-four hours? "Gwen?"

"I'm sorry to bother you—so I won't keep you but a minute—but I need to tell Mrs. Gray what time to serve dinner this evening. Is seven all right?"

"I'll just grab something on the way home, so…"

"I'm afraid that's not going to work." Gwen sighed. "I'd hoped to talk to you about this last night at dinner but you were, um, called away before I could."

Gwen sounded irritated. Evie must be giving her problems. "And?"

"If you want Evie to make progress, she's going to need to practice. But she needs to practice with someone other than just me, and dinner is a perfect time. Every night would be best, but you'll need to be home every other night at least."

"I'm very busy—"

"I know, but we only have three weeks until the Med Ball. Do you or do you not want Evie to be ready?"

"Of course I want her to be ready—"

"Then we'll see you at dinner. Seven o'clock. Goodbye, Will."

His hackles went up. Who did she think she was? *She* worked for *him*. He buzzed Nancy with the intention of having her get Miss Behavior back on the line so he could get a few things straight about this arrangement…

An unfamiliar feeling stopped him. This was important for Evie; therefore, it was important to him. And what would it hurt after all? It would only be for a couple of weeks, and Mrs. Gray's meals were a lot better than the take-away bistro on the corner.

"Yes, Mr. Harrison?"

"Find Mitchell and move our meeting back to five o'clock. I have to be out of here no later than six-thirty today."

"Of course."

"And, Nancy?"

"Yes, Mr. Harrison?"

He could not believe he was doing this. "Go through my

appointment book and reschedule any meeting in the next three weeks that will run later than six."

"Um…" He could hear the confusion in her voice, but she caught herself quickly. "Not a problem."

Oh, it would be one hell of a problem. His schedule simply wasn't that flexible. But he'd be able to assess Evie's progress and report back to Marcus on a regular basis.

And seeing Gwen in action wouldn't be bad, either.

"Sometimes, the dessert spoon will be above the plate, along with a dessert fork."

Evie looked confused for the thousandth time, but Gwen was pleased that she didn't show her frustration.

"So how's that different from the soup spoon?"

"Silver is always placed in the order it will be used. Start at the outside and work your way in with each course." At Evie's disgruntled look, Gwen added, "And you can always pause for a moment and wait to see which utensil everyone else picks up."

"No, I can do this." With her back ramrod straight and a determined set to her chin, Evie went over the place setting again. Granted, Gwen's teaching set contained enough pieces for the most formal of dinners—far more than Evie would ever be faced with unless she attended a state dinner at Buckingham Palace—but it didn't hurt to cover every possible base. From past experience, Gwen knew that if Evie felt like she had this under control, any regular setting would seem like child's play.

"Red wine, white wine, champagne, water. My glasses are to the right." She touched each piece as she spoke. "Fish fork, salad fork, dinner fork, bread plate and butter knife—"

"Good God, what are we having for dinner?"

Gwen looked up to see Will standing in the doorway, tie loosened and his briefcase still in his hand.

Evie paused in her recitation. "Baked chicken and green

beans." Without waiting for a response, she continued. "Service plate, soup bowl, soup spoon, oyster fork…"

Gwen stepped from behind Evie's chair. "It's a teaching set. Every possible fork she might come across. I think Mrs. Gray will let us slide with a smaller setting for tonight."

She caught the amused smile playing at the corners of Will's mouth. "Well, that's good to know."

"Hey, Will, did you know there's a special fork just for oysters? I always thought you just picked them up and slurped them out, but Gwen says that's not the proper thing to do. Did you know that?"

"I think slurping of any sort is against the rules. But how you'd get the slippery little suckers onto a fork is beyond me." Over Evie's giggle, he added, "I'm going to take Gwen in the other room for a probably well-deserved drink while you check with Mrs. Gray about what forks she does need on the table."

Evie balked, and Gwen wondered if she'd ever help set a table before. A look from Will sent her scurrying for the kitchen.

"I'll come get you guys when it's time to eat."

"A drink, Gwen?"

"I'd love one, but not because Evie's driven me to it. She's done very well today."

"That's good to hear." Will stepped back and indicated she should lead the way. In the hallway, Will dropped his briefcase on a side table and fell into step beside her. She gasped as his hand went to the small of her back, the warmth seeping through her shirt to heat her skin. She swayed, her balance suddenly off-kilter.

It's just a polite gesture, nothing more. Still, the shock propelled her the last few feet into the living room and away from his touch.

She took a seat on the long, butter-soft leather sofa and watched as Will poured two glasses of wine from the bar. He handed her a glass and stepped away. She took a sip, glad to see her equilibrium had returned with distance.

Will seemed unaware of her discomfort. He took the wing chair opposite her and relaxed against its back. "I've never seen someone so excited about oyster forks and soup spoons."

"Evie's just eager to please right now. Everything is new and, therefore, fun. It'll pass in a few days. Believe me."

"So you're settled in okay?" He ran a hand through his hair, leaving it standing in funny spikes. She was still having problems reconciling the Will Harrison from the papers with the one she was seeing in person. The corporate CEO didn't mesh with the man in front of her, the one who sputtered at the sight of a formal place setting and teased his little sister about oysters.

"Yes, thank you. Your home is lovely." Funny, this room felt smaller than it did when she and Evie were in here earlier. *Polite small talk. Come on, Miss Behavior, you can do small talk.* She took another sip of her wine. "Did you have a good day?"

"I guess you could call it that." Will removed his tie completely and tossed it over the arm of the chair before unbuttoning the top three buttons of his white dress shirt, exposing bronze skin underneath. Although Will continued talking, she wasn't able to concentrate on his words. *Definitely some kind of outdoor activity.* The lack of a tan line at the base of his throat meant whatever he did outside, he did it shirtless.

Pull it together. She had no business pondering his shirt-free activities—whatever they might be. She should have known after her reaction to him in his office yesterday that moving in to such close proximity would be a very bad idea. Then she'd compounded the problem by insisting he be home every night for dinner. How long before he fired her for gawking at him? Not only was it extremely bad manners—and she should know—but it was unprofessional as well.

This adolescent mooning had to stop. She was *not* going down that path again. She'd learned that lesson the hard way. Or at least she thought she had. Obviously her libido was a bit of a slow learner. Maybe it was just because she'd been in a bit of a dating dry spell recently.

Fine. The day after the Med Ball she'd start dating again. She'd let Sarah set her up, hit the bars, try an online site— anything. She just needed to make it until then *without* making a fool of herself again.

Focus on Evie, and try to forget about her brother. Easier said than done, when even as she promised herself she'd find a man soon, she could still feel his hand on the small of her back like a brand.

Will sat on the balcony, his legs stretched out on the railing and a drink in his hand. The lights of Dallas spread out in front of him, twinkling in the darkness.

Evie and Gwen were both in their rooms and Mrs. Gray had long since gone home, and the apartment had fallen silent. At first, the quiet felt odd; he kept expecting to hear Evie's stereo or Mrs. Gray banging pots and pans in the kitchen. Funny how quickly he'd adjusted to having people around— Evie, Mrs. Gray and now, Gwen.

The balcony off Gwen's room angled his, and the glow from behind her curtains meant she was still awake. He'd heard the unmistakable click of computer keys as he walked by earlier. Was she a workaholic, taking advantage of the quiet evening to answer the etiquette questions of the country's youth? If he knocked on her door, would she join him for a drink on the balcony instead?

When he'd opened the front door, he'd heard Evie's reci- tation of flatware and gone to the dining room expecting to find Miss Behavior in full form. He'd been struck speechless instead. Gwen's sensible suit had disappeared, replaced by a simple sundress that flowed over her curves intriguingly. Her hair hung loose around her shoulders, and as she'd passed him in the hallway, he'd caught a faint whiff of lavender.

The scent suited her: elegant, a bit old-fashioned and very feminine. He'd breathed deep and the residual tension of his day eased away. And while Gwen seemed to stay slightly on edge as they chatted, he'd found the wine to be an unnecessary additional relaxant.

He'd been charmed by her at dinner. When he agreed to be home for more family meals, he hadn't expected to enjoy it so much. Evie's presence seemed to melt some of the reserve he normally felt from Gwen, and he found her to be well-read and refreshing in her opinions.

And Evie! Gwen may have said it was too early to tell, but he could see the changes in Evie already. She did have natural charm, and under Gwen's gentle guidance, she was learning how to use it.

The light in Gwen's room went dark, and he'd missed his chance to offer her a nightcap.

It was probably just as well—getting involved with his sister's tutor in any way could only cause problems. If he'd learned nothing else from his father's late-life love affair, he certainly knew the folly of fishing in the company pond. At least the various women Marcus kept pushing at him as potential partners would never cause the same embarrassment Rachel had. They had their own wealth, their own family connections—they didn't need his in order to climb the social ladder.

Nope, he was better off enjoying the evening alone.

Then why did he have this lingering regret he hadn't asked her earlier?

CHAPTER THREE

THIS was definitely the way to work.

The guest room of Will's penthouse had its own private balcony, and Gwen had taken her laptop outside. Looking over the railing from almost twenty floors up had made her feel dizzy, but as long as she stayed away from the railing, she was fine. The small table and chairs had enough room for her computer and paperwork, and she could enjoy the summer breezes while she worked.

Mrs. Gray brought her a small pot of tea and some snacks about the time Evie went downstairs for her tennis lesson, and the apartment was quiet except for the jazz floating from the CD player inside in her bedroom. She loved her little 1920's cottage and the charm of M Street, but *this* she could get used to.

She posted her column to TeenSpace and answered a few e-mails. For the most part, she'd been able to either postpone clients or move them to the blocks of time she knew Evie would be with her tutors or at a lesson, but she'd sent a few to a friend and former classmate who did some deb training on the side. The obnoxious sum of money Will was paying her for this job more than covered the loss of income from those few classes.

She was just shutting down her laptop when her cell phone rang.

"You never called yesterday and I'm dying to hear *everything*." Her sister sounded as eager as Evie.

"I know. I was busy getting settled in, and Evie and I worked most of the day." The breeze on the balcony made it hard to hear Sarah, so she went inside and flopped on the sinfully wonderful bed.

"And…"

"The guest room here is nicer than that five-star hotel we stayed at in D.C. last year. The bathroom is the size of my bedroom at home and done completely in marble. The bedroom is huge, and I have my own balcony. It's *incredible*."

"Even the hired help lives the good life, huh?"

"That's for sure." Gwen rolled on to her back, felt the down duvet mold itself around her and stared at the hand-painted ceiling. "I swear, I feel like a princess in this room."

"What about the princess herself?"

"Evie's not bad at all. A little unsure of herself and the finer points of etiquette, but she's far from the mess I expected. I'm going to bring her in Friday, if that's still okay. I think you'll like her."

"Friday's fine. E-mail me her picture and sizes. Now, quit stalling and tell me about the Most Eligible Will Harrison."

Gwen nibbled on a fingernail as she hedged. "There's not much to tell."

"Gwennie!" Sisterly exasperation took over. "Details. Now. I'm holding your cat hostage, you know."

"Okay, okay. He's even more handsome than his pictures, and he can be quite charming when he wants to. Trust me, charm is not something the Harrison family lacks." So it wasn't the full truth, but Sarah wasn't ready to hear that Gwen was living with a man who oozed sex appeal. And she wasn't about to go into the details of what that was doing to her equilibrium. "He's really good to Evie, too, even though they're still figuring each other out."

"I hear a 'but.'"

"*But* he's terse sometimes and always seems to be thinking about something else when I'm talking to him. And if that damn BlackBerry rings one more time, I'll—"

Sarah's sigh interrupted her rant. "Not everyone feels the way you do about phones, Gwen. He's probably a very busy man. BlackBerrys just come with the territory."

It was her turn to be exasperated. "You know good and well that flesh and blood people—"

"'Always take priority over any message in any other medium.' Yes, Gwennie, I know. That speech is getting old, honey."

"That doesn't make it any less true." She knew she sounded huffy and defensive, but she also knew Sarah had been brought up better than that.

"Maybe you should work on some new etiquette rules for *this* century."

"The ones we have would work just fine if folks would only follow them." Sarah started to interrupt again, but Gwen cut her off. "He brought it to dinner."

"Oh." Even Sarah's lax rules on technology use included a moratorium on their presence at the dinner table. Mother had taught them too well. "So Will Harrison needs some work in the cell phone etiquette department. Big deal. He's handsome and charming and richer than God. You can overlook a couple of flaws."

"Sarah, I have no business even noticing his flaws. *Evie* Harrison is my business, not Will." *That needs to become my new mantra.*

"So? You're there. Living in his house. You're both adults, and you never know…"

Sarah was going to drive her insane. "Forty-eight hours ago you were telling me what a bad idea moving in here was. You've switched camps pretty suddenly."

"I just wanted to make sure you'd thought this whole thing through. Now that you're there…" She trailed off suggestively. "Anyway, you said you felt like this was the right thing to do. That it was your chance. Maybe it is in more ways than one. Couldn't hurt to keep your options open."

"You're jumping *way* ahead. Granted, Will is absolutely yummy—"

Sarah perked up. "Yummy? Really?"

Oh, for a different choice of words. Too late now. "This is business—and the future of my business. As you said, I've laid a lot of groundwork the last few years. I'm not going to screw everything up again with some silly crush on my boss."

"So he *is* crushworthy."

Gwen wanted to bury her head in the pillows and scream. "This whole conversation is ridiculous. Will Harrison barely knows I'm alive. I'm just someone he hired to tutor his sister. I doubt Evie's French teacher is having this conversation with *her* siblings."

"He didn't ask the French teacher to move in, now did he?"

Gwen heard the front door slam and the pounding of feet in the hallway. *Perfect timing.* She sent up a quick word of thanks. "Evie's back from her tennis lesson. I need to go."

"But you haven't told me anything—"

"I've *got* to go. Miss Behavior duty. We're going to work on introductions and handshakes this afternoon."

"Oooh, fun."

"Sarcasm isn't becoming of a lady, you know. Neither is that," she added as Sarah made a raspberry noise in her ear. She heard Evie call her name as footsteps approached her room. "I'll see you Friday, okay?"

"This conversation isn't over, you know."

"Yes, it is."

"At least think about what I said. Don't let past mistakes color your perception and cause you to miss out on an opportunity."

"Past mistakes are what's keeping my perception crystal clear." Sarah started to grumble again. To keep the peace she added, "But I'll think about what you said. Bye." She flipped her phone closed before Sarah had a chance to argue some more.

Sarah went through life like it was some kind of movie—which, for her, it often was. Gwen just needed to remind herself of that so that her sister wouldn't drive her into therapy or cause her to lose her job. If she limited her calls to Sarah over the next couple of weeks, she'd be able to concentrate much better on the job at hand.

Head in the game. Eyes on the prize. Hands to herself.

That should be easy enough to remember.

"*Konichiwa*." His tongue felt too thick to get the word out sounding anything like the voice on the computer lesson. Picking up Japanese in three weeks would be a challenge.

He looked over the notes Nancy had prepared about doing business with the Japanese. The business card thing was no problem; bowing wasn't that difficult to figure out. But he'd read how making an effort to learn a few words of Japanese—however badly pronounced—would go a long way in creating good feelings.

And good feelings were much needed. Expanding HarCorp's distribution of its luxury items into Asian markets had been his personal goal for the company for the last three years.

HarCorp's background was tied in Texas cattle, but the Harrison family didn't have ranch roots. His great-grandfather opened one of the first tanneries in the area, providing leather to the saddle and boot makers. When the demand for saddles waned, Harrison Tannery changed its name and began supplying leather to the automakers and eventually began supplying leather overseas as well.

The Luxury Goods arm of HarCorp had been a special project of Will's since he joined the family business. He'd championed it when the entire board had tried to nix the idea. It wasn't until his father retired that he was able to give it the attention it deserved, but Luxury Goods now showed a larger profit than any other department, and the naysayers were off his back. Now that Harrison Leathers had made a name for itself providing unique, high-quality items, it was time to expand their reach to the newly affluent Asian countries and their growing upper classes. Kiesuke Hiramine was his way into that market. The meeting scheduled for next month would be the make-or-break moment of three years' hard work.

"*Konichiwa,*" he tried again. "*Dochirahe.*"

The intercom on his desk beeped. "Mr. Harrison, are you ready for me now?"

He glanced at his watch. Three-thirty already, and past time for his daily meeting with his assistant. "Come on in, Nancy."

One second later, Nancy knocked sharply on his door and entered. With her usual efficiency—and he paid her handsomely for it—she went through his calendar and schedule for the immediate future as he signed the stack of papers she laid on his desk.

"Finally *Dallas Lifestyles* would like to know if you can schedule an interview and photo shoot."

A snort escaped at the mention of the magazine. Four-color gossip on glossy paper was still trash, no matter how the magazine tried to promote itself as something other than a gossip rag. He looked up from the contract he was initialing to see the corner of Nancy's mouth twitching in amusement. "Why on earth would I do that?"

Nancy feigned a look of innocence. "It's part of the whole 'Dallas's Most Eligible' package. Each Bachelor gets a spread. You're the only one left—are you sure you don't want to schedule?"

"Has hell frozen over yet?" That's all he needed: *more* encouragement for the fortune-hunting women out there on the dating circuit. Like he didn't have enough on his plate already between running HarCorp and raising Evie. Even if he had the inclination, he certainly didn't have the time.

"That's what I thought. But I told them I'd ask anyway. Maybe they'll quit calling now," she grumbled.

"We can hope, right?"

Nancy shrugged as she collected the now-signed papers from his desk. Knowing they were finished, Will turned back to his computer and clicked the file on Japanese business etiquette open again. He needed to figure out this bowing thing.

"Anything else I can do for you?"

He laughed but didn't take his eyes off the screen. "Yeah. Find me a Japanese expert to run my meeting."

His intercom on his desk beeped, meaning the lobby receptionist wanted to put a call directly through—which meant the call was either from Evie or Marcus. Nancy left as he answered.

"Hi, Will. I'm sorry to bother you."

Hearing Gwen's voice caught him off-guard. Jewel, the executive receptionist, must have been told something about their situation in order for Gwen to get connected to him directly. He hadn't thought about doing it, but Nancy obviously had.

"It's no bother." Surprisingly he meant that. "Is everything all right?"

"Oh, yes. Everything's fine. Marcus Heatherton called Evie today to say he'll be here for dinner tonight."

He'd forgotten about that. "I guess I should have warned you. Marcus is checking up on us."

"On me, you mean." He could hear the smile in her voice. Gwen was sharp.

"How'd you know?"

"After everything Evie's told me, I'm surprised he's waited this long." She sounded amused at the situation, which surprised *him*. Marcus was well-known, and it wasn't for his laid-back outlook on life. Surely Gwen had at least heard of him in dealing with her debutantes.

His computer beeped, signaling an incoming e-mail. He glanced at the message and shot back a quick response.

"Mrs. Gray, however, is all atwitter. Something about Mr. Heatherton being impossible to please."

"Oh, well, there was that one night when the meat was a little tough…"

"So, it's going to be an interesting evening then." Gwen chuckled conspiratorially, and the sound was infectious. He liked this side of her. Gwen still seemed tense whenever he was around, and this was one of the few times he'd felt her loosening up.

"Oh, definitely."

"Actually I wanted to tell you that Mr. Heatherton plans to arrive around six-thirty. I'm hoping you'll be able to make it home a bit earlier tonight. I think he's eager to see you."

That comment brought a full-out laugh. "You *have* heard of Marcus. Don't worry. I'll be home in plenty of time to run interference for you."

"That's not what I was implying—"

"Yes it was." This was fun. How long had it been since he'd had an enjoyable and somewhat normal conversation with a woman? Years, possibly. He eased back in his chair and propped his feet on the desk. "Marcus will be nothing if not impressed by you—what you've done with Evie, that is."

"I hope. Evie's a bit nervous. You did tell her she wasn't going to be sent to boarding school, right?"

"Yep." His e-mail beeped again, and he glanced at the subject line. As much as he was enjoying the conversation, it was time to get back to it. "Anything else I can do for you— short of uninviting Marcus to dinner?"

"Actually there is one more thing. You mentioned before that you wanted me to help Evie with her wardrobe. I'll be taking her to Neiman Marcus tomorrow."

Money. Of course. Everything in his life always came back to money. *His* money. Not that he minded spending it on Evie, but Gwen bringing it up had kind of dampened the mood. For a moment there, he'd forgotten he'd bought her time and attention. Her attention to Evie, he meant. "I'll take care of it. Anything else?"

"Guess not. We'll see you tonight." He heard Evie's voice in the background then Gwen's muffled voice as she placed a hand over the phone to answer her. "Oh, Will?"

His intercom was beeping. He didn't have time for this. "Yes?"

"Evie says not to be late. Mr. Heatherton frowns on tardiness, and it would be rude." That restrained laughter in her voice snared him again.

"Tell Evie I said she has to wear a dress." He waited as Gwen relayed the message and heard Evie's wail in response. The intercom's beeping got more insistent. "I have to go. I'll see you tonight."

He switched to the intercom line to find Nancy waiting impatiently. "Mr. Hiramine's assistant is on line three."

"Great. Tamishi, right?"

"No, Takeshi."

"Thanks. And tell Davis to just e-mail the sales figures. I have dinner arrangements with Marcus tonight, and I'll look them over at home. I'll be leaving early today."

Nancy's surprise registered, but he didn't have time to explain further.

"*Konichiwa,* Takeshi."

CHAPTER FOUR

"PAUL ANGERON tells me your backhand is showing great improvement, Evangeline." Marcus Heatherton wiped his small white beard with a monogrammed napkin and leveled a proud smile at Evie.

Evie brightened as she launched into a spirited rendition of the former Wimbledon winner's description of her tennis prowess. Gwen lowered her eyes to the table and hid a smile of her own. Evie had Mr. Heatherton eating out of the palm of her hand. A quick glance at Will and his half smile confirmed her thought.

Mrs. Gray had pulled out all the stops for dinner—once she'd finished grumbling, at least. Although the courses were uncomplicated, the food was plated beautifully on gold-rimmed china. The cream linen and the gleaming crystal seemed a bit over the top for a family dinner of salmon and potatoes, but Mrs. Gray had insisted Evie needed the full effect for this evening.

All of Evie's worries that Mr. Heatherton would find something wrong with her manners seemed to have evaporated. Although she still dominated the conversation a bit more than was correct, she hadn't interrupted anyone and proved she could tell an entertaining story for her guests.

No question about it. Evie was going to be fine.

Will's laugh brought her back to the conversation, and she

wondered what she'd missed with her woolgathering. Some etiquette tutor she was—mentally wandering away from a conversation was plain rude and she knew better. If only the Harrisons didn't give her so much to think about.

With Evie, she had an excuse—it was her job to correct, encourage, evaluate and decide what step was next in the run up to Evie's presence at the Hospital Med Ball. As for Will... well, she had no excuse other than her own unusual fascination with the man. In some ways, he was exactly the man she'd expected—businesslike, busy and often distant. More often than not, she found herself unsure of what to say or do when around him. Plus, she couldn't decide if his occasional rudeness and incessant BlackBerry usage was deliberate or not.

Regardless, she even found it difficult to follow her cardinal rule of "maintain eye contact," because staring into Will Harrison's eyes could turn any woman into brain-dead mush. And if he smiled...Lord, the man should carry a warning label. Plus he could also be kind and funny and completely approachable at times. Like when...

"Gwen?"

She looked up to see everyone watching her. Mr. Heatherton's frown had returned at her inattention. Evie stared at her openly in mild shock, and Gwen could practically hear her own lecture about attentiveness to others replaying in Evie's head. Will simply looked amused for some reason. She cleared her throat as she felt her cheeks heat. "I'm so sorry. I was thinking about Evie's shopping trip tomorrow."

"Gwen's sister is a buyer at Neiman Marcus. We'll be getting my wardrobe up to scratch. What color dress do you think would be most appropriate for the Med Ball, Uncle Marcus?"

"White or pastels, my dear. You're much too young for anything else. And remember who you are—avoid anything flashy..."

She could kiss Evie for that save. Whatever question Mr. Heatherton had asked her was forgotten as he launched into a lecture on the horrid state of formal wear for young women. Evie was doing an admirable job of hanging on every word like he was the Fashion Oracle of Dallas.

Hearing a small snort of laughter from her right, Gwen looked over to see Will pretending to study his meal carefully. Without making eye contact, he leaned slightly toward her and whispered, "Tsk, tsk, Miss Behavior."

Buttering her roll kept her from winging it in Will's direction. Instead she waited until Will looked her way and winked at him. His eyebrows went up in surprise then, to *her* surprise, she felt his foot nudge hers under the table.

She nudged his foot in response, but Will had focused his attention on Marcus and seemed engrossed in his lecture on the importance of a modest neckline.

When Evie nudged her foot from the other side, Gwen's head snapped in her direction only to feel Will's foot reach over hers to nudge Evie's. She almost laughed out loud. Both Harrisons wore looks of absorbed interest on their faces while they kicked each other under the table like children.

Who knew Will Harrison could be playful enough to foot-fight with his sister under the dinner table? For the sake of Evie's education, she should put a stop to it, but there was no real harm. Marcus seemed completely unaware.

Another nudge from Will. This time Gwen retaliated more forcefully, only to miss her target and connect with the center table leg instead. Glassware rattled, and Marcus paused midsentence.

Oh, no. The heat returned to her cheeks.

"Sorry, everyone." Will covered for her smoothly, earning him a frown from Marcus and Gwen's eternal gratitude.

This was just dandy. She could hear her mother's voice chiding her for her behavior. Enough was enough. Time for her to remember she was a grown-up and act like one.

She cleared her throat. "Mr. Heatherton, will you be attending the Med Ball this year?"

"Of course, my dear. I try to attend every year, if only to put in an appearance. This year, however, it will be my pleasure to introduce Bradley's beautiful daughter to friends of the family." He patted Evie's hand fondly.

Evie beamed at the indirect acknowledgment of her social skills, but Marcus moved on.

"And you, William, will you be escorting Grace Myerly?"

Evie's eyes were as wide as Gwen's felt as they both looked at Will, who seemed to be having difficulty swallowing his salmon all of a sudden. Gwen thought she was up-to-date on all the society doings just by listening to her debs' conversations, but she didn't recall hearing Will's name connected to the great paragon Grace Myerly before.

"No, Grace and I aren't seeing each other any longer."

"That's a shame. You made such a lovely couple, and your families go way back."

She was still processing the Will and Grace connection when Mr. Heatherton turned his attention to her.

"Gwen, you know the Myerly family don't you?"

Gwen sat up straight. "Yes, I do. Not socially, of course, but both of the younger Myerly girls were in my debutante classes several years ago."

"Of course. Lovely girls, both of them."

If you say so. Personally Gwen felt the youngest Myerlys were spoiled, self-absorbed brats who'd made her classes hell for all involved. The older Myerlys hadn't helped the situation with their own self-important attitude. She was glad there weren't any other Myerly children at home ready to debut.

She nodded instead. "I haven't met Grace before, although I do know who she is." Everyone knew Grace Myerly. The woman was constantly in the papers for her charity work and her fabulous parties. Tall, willowy, gorgeous and seemingly gracious, she was the epitome of Southern high class and, by all standards, the perfect type of woman for Will.

Something unpleasant coiled in her stomach.

"Why don't you take Gwen, Will?" Evie piped up with that idea, sending Marcus's fork clattering to his plate. Will froze, his eyes locking on Gwen's face with a "Fix This" look, but she was too busy choking on her wine to do anything.

Evie, however, was oblivious to the change in atmosphere: "That way, Gwen can help keep me from messing up, and you won't have to deal with—what did you call it?—'the desperate cling of ageing socialites.'" When no one spoke, Evie looked at each face closely. "What? What's the problem?"

Evie looked genuinely confused. Will wanted to help, but wasn't sure he knew where to start. Marcus looked horrified, and Will knew at any moment Marcus would say something snobbish or classist and make the situation worse.

The grandfather clock in the hallway ticked in the silence as tears gathered in the corners of Evie's eyes because she didn't understand the currents swirling around her.

Gwen recovered first and placed her hand over Evie's. Will remembered that look on her face from their first meeting— the moment had passed and Gwen was back in charge. She'd know exactly the right thing to say.

He couldn't *wait* to hear it.

"Evie, honey, it's not appropriate to ask one person to ask another person to a social function like that. It puts everyone in an uncomfortable situation." Gwen's voice was gentle, with no trace of censure. "It puts Will in the position of asking me or risk insulting me or hurting my feelings, when he may have someone else in mind to ask. I take the risk of hurting his feelings if I have to say 'no' for whatever reason, plus it's embarrassing for the people involved to have such personal matters discussed in front of others. Understand?"

Evie nodded.

Bravo, Gwen.

"Remember, one of the most important purposes of etiquette is to make everyone feel comfortable and at ease. Quizzing people about their dating habits or trying to fix them up on a date never makes anyone feel at ease."

And that reminder was for you, Marcus. Score two points for Miss Behavior. Hopefully Marcus wouldn't bring up the topic of Grace Myerly again. It was only luck this time that sidetracked the conversation before Marcus had Will and Grace combining HarCorp and Myerly Cattle into one large family empire. Marcus and Peter Myerly had been pushing shallow, bubbleheaded Grace at him since Grace's debut.

If Gwen *had* intended that remark for Marcus however, she didn't show it. She seemed fully focused on Evie.

As Evie opened her mouth to say something more, Gwen's expression changed from one of cool calm to an unmistakable "We'll discuss this later." Evie nodded again in understanding, then turned her mother's megawatt smile on everyone.

"I see, and I'm very sorry if I made you all uncomfortable."

Gwen adeptly steered the conversation in a new direction, and the moment seemed forgotten. Marcus was soon pontificating on something—Will lost the thread quickly—and Evie and Gwen nodded in all the right places.

A weight lifted from his shoulders. Gwen was a godsend. Marcus was pleased. Evie was a new person—in three days, Gwen had not only improved her manners exponentially, but Evie seemed to be smiling more. For the first time in weeks, he really felt like this whole situation would work out. Nancy would be getting a nice surprise in her next paycheck for delivering Miss Behavior to his front door.

As Mrs. Gray served dessert and coffee, he nudged Gwen's foot under the table again, and smiled his thanks. Gwen seemed to understand.

His BlackBerry chirped, indicating an e-mail. Probably Davis's sales report finally arriving. He fished it out of his pocket to check.

"You're not supposed to do that, Will." Evie's voice stopped him before he could open the message. He looked up to see Evie shaking her head at him in censure. He heard Gwen's shocked "Evie!" but Evie continued.

"Gwen says you're not supposed to have cell phones and stuff at the dinner table. It's rude to put technology before people. Right, Gwen?" Evie turned to Gwen for confirmation.

Gwen looked completely ill at ease.

Belatedly Will realized Evie—and by extension, Gwen—was right. He'd lived alone for so long, he'd gotten into lots of bad habits. He slid the BlackBerry back into his pocket and opened his mouth to apologize.

Marcus beat him to the punch. "Evangeline, William is a very busy man and the business needs his attention."

He tried to jump in. "Evie, I—"

"But Gwen says the rules apply to everybody all the time. It doesn't matter who they are."

Gwen went slightly pale. "Evie, we don't correct others."

"But you correct me all the time."

"That's because it's my job. What's rude is to correct other people in social situations. *Especially* your elders," she whispered.

"But, Gwen…" Evie's cheeks were getting flushed.

Marcus adjusted his cuffs and leaned forward. "Evangeline—"

"Why does everyone get to tell me what to do and tell me how wrong I am when they're breaking rules too? Will has his BlackBerry, Uncle Marcus is holding his fork wrong, and I'm the one getting yelled at!"

She had a point. She also had their father's famous temper, and that he knew how to deal with.

"Evie…"

But Evie carefully placed her napkin on the table and pushed her chair back. As she stood, he saw her take a deep breath to control herself. "Uncle Marcus, Will, I apologize for losing my temper and being rude. If you'll excuse me, I have a headache and need to go lie down. Good night, everyone."

With that, she stomped from the room. Moments later, he heard her bedroom door slam.

Silence followed her departure. Gwen looked shocked and Marcus was frowning again.

With an attempt at levity, he said, "Well, she's certainly learned the art of the dramatic exit." *And a little bit of Gwen's "extreme politeness" trick.*

Gwen seemed to be calling on that same trick. "My apologies as well. If you'll excuse me, I'll go talk to Evie."

He caught her hand as she tried to rise and a little zing of electricity shot through him. The way her eyes snapped up to his had him wondering if she'd felt it, too. "Leave her alone for a little while. She needs to calm down first."

Marcus chuckled, and Will got to watch Gwen's jaw drop in shock. "She has the Harrison temper, that's for sure. William's right, Gwen. I've dealt with this before myself—with both Bradley and William, mind you. She'll need to stew for a while before she can calm down. There's no use trying to talk to a Harrison while they're angry." With that, Marcus pushed his own chair back from the table.

"But I'll leave you two to sort that out." He reached for Gwen's hand and shook it warmly. "It was a pleasure to meet you, my dear. You're doing a wonderful job with Evangeline."

Will walked Marcus to the door. "I must say, William, that's the most interesting dinner I've had with you in years."

"You can say that again."

When he returned to the dining room, he found Gwen gathering plates from the table while Mrs. Gray clucked at her to stop.

"Come on, Gwen. I'll get you a drink and we'll sit on the balcony."

She followed him to the other room but declined the glass he offered. *Guess a trip to the balcony is out, too.* Gwen didn't sit, either. Instead she gripped her hands in front of her and straightened her spine as she faced him.

"I'm sorry about that, Will. Really. I expected her to blow

at some point…I just didn't mean for it to happen in front of you and Mr. Heatherton. I figured she'd take it out on me."

"You were expecting that?"

She nodded. "It's hard to have someone correct you all the time. How you walk, how you talk, how you hold your glass. Having every move you make critiqued and never getting it quite right." She laughed, but it was a bitter sound. "It gets old really fast. Trust me on this. I know how Evie feels."

There was a story there, but he had the feeling Gwen wouldn't want to go any deeper in to it, so he didn't ask. He'd guess Miss Behavior hadn't always gotten the forks right.

He sat and invited her to do the same. To his surprise—and pleasure—she chose to sit on the sofa with him.

"Believe me, though, when I say Evie will do fine—at the Med Ball and in general."

"I know she will. Like Marcus said, Evie really is showing great improvement. I'm very—I mean we're very pleased. Marcus said it was the most interesting dinner he's had here."

Gwen's shoulders slumped in what might be relief and she sagged back against the arm of the sofa before she caught herself and straightened back up. "Interesting is one way to put it."

"Go ahead and relax. You've earned it." She had. Evie's outburst aside, the evening had been a success, and he owed that to Gwen. "We'll let Miss Behavior take the rest of the night off, and we'll talk about something else."

Relax? He had to be kidding. She'd just experienced one of the strangest dinners of her career—make that her life—and he expected her to relax? The Harrisons were going to drive her insane.

She hadn't lied when she said she'd been expecting Evie's outburst, but when she'd snapped there at the table, Gwen thought her heart would stop beating. When Evie pointed out Mr. Heatherton's fork problems, she'd had a clear vision of her career going up in a puff of smoke. Again. And this time, it wouldn't even be her fault.

But both Marcus and Will seemed to have taken it all in good humor, and while it was a relief, it wasn't doing much for her nerves. And sitting this close to him on the sofa wasn't helping her composure, either. The easy smile caused adorable crinkles around his eyes and brought that devastating dimple out to play hell with her equilibrium. The deep breath she took to try to calm herself backfired when the spicy scent of his aftershave coiled through her and tied her stomach in an aroused knot.

Now he wanted her to have a drink and talk about something other than Evie and etiquette. What did that leave? HarCorp? She doubted he'd believe an interest in the actual business, and there wasn't exactly a casual way to broach the topic of her corporate workshops. No, her career had already teetered on the edge once this evening. There was no sense flirting with disaster again by bringing up *that*. The weather? Politics? Every topic of small talk fled her head as Will shifted to a more comfortable position and treated her to a full-out, heart-stopping smile.

"Are you sure I can't get you a drink? Wine?"

Was Will flirting with her? A drink? On the balcony? Small talk? Her stomach fluttered at the thrill before common sense stamped it down. She worked for him, and she wouldn't believe for a second he flirted with his employees. Of course, this wasn't a normal employment situation, what with her moving in and all. Maybe...

Oh, no, she was doing it again. How stupid could one person be? She'd been down this path before, and it had ended in disaster, heartbreak, professional disgrace... None of which she planned on repeating. Sarah's little fantasy must have tripped some switch in her brain, turning her back into a complete idiot who let her libido lead her. She needed to put this evening back on its professional feet, and she racked her brain for an appropriate, *neutral* topic.

Will was saying something, but her heart thudded in her ears, drowning out his words as he leaned toward her. The couch seemed to shrink, moving him closer to her, and the temperature in the room rose several degrees. How'd she end up so close to him? So close she could see his eyes darken?

Her heartbeat accelerated. Rational thoughts clamored to be heard, but were easily brushed aside as those hazel eyes swept over her, affecting her senses as strongly as a caress.

When his hand reached out to gently brush her arm, she felt the hairs rise from the electricity before he even touched her.

"Gwen?"

The question was a whisper, his lips just inches from hers, and instead of answering, she let her eyes slide closed in response.

"Will? Gwen? Where are you guys?"

Evie's voice snapped them apart and sent them to opposite ends of the sofa moments before her head peered around the corner.

Damn, damn, double damn. Her heart was racing—from desire or adrenaline, she didn't know. While her hormones protested at the interruption, the logical, rational part of her brain kicked back in and sent up a word of thanks at Evie's perfect timing.

Evie looked confused. "Did I interrupt something?"

Only my latest attempt at career suicide.

Will coughed and dragged a hand through his hair. Gwen gave herself a strong mental shake and plastered a serene smile on her face. "Of course not."

"I came to apologize. For losing my temper, I mean. I hope I didn't ruin dinner for everyone." After a small pause, she added, "Is Uncle Marcus mad?"

Gwen decided to leave this opening to Will. He was the "parent" in this situation, after all, and she was just the hired help. *Remember that, Gwennie.*

"No one's mad at you. We were just a bit shocked. You will

need to guard that temper of yours in the future, though. It might not fly well in the dining room of the Club."

Gwen simply nodded her agreement.

"But, Will, you know I'm right. You shouldn't have your BlackBerry at the table. If I have to behave, so do you."

Gwen cleared her throat, desperate for the chance to escape. "Um, I find that I'm really exhausted all of a sudden, and since Evie and I have a big day tomorrow, I'm going to head on to bed." She wanted to be out of there before Evie left; there was no way she was ready to deal with what almost happened. She then rushed for the safety of her bedroom before either Harrison could say anything.

That had been close. Too close.

CHAPTER FIVE

TAKING Evie shopping had seemed like such a good idea at the time. She'd even enjoyed the morning's activities—haircuts, manicures, pedicures, lunch in the Neiman Marcus restaurant. Evie's need for female companionship and her obvious enjoyment of such a girly day out kept a smile on Gwen's face.

But that almost-but-not-quite moment of the night before kept haunting her. She might have had more Will-free thoughts if Evie could go longer than ten minutes without mentioning him. Or if Evie didn't share so many mannerisms with Will that a tilt of her head or a certain phrase didn't make her think of him.

It was bad enough she'd spent hours staring at the ceiling last night replaying each and every second of her entire short history with Will in her head, trying to figure out when her professional working relationship with the man had veered wildly off-track. Spending the morning trying not to moon over the man while still spending time with his sister…well, that was a new exercise in personal torture.

And the torture wasn't over yet. The instant connection between her young charge and her sister should have clued her in. Their kindred shopping spirits recognized each other instantly, and Gwen resigned herself to a very long afternoon.

Sarah had commandeered a private room normally reserved by the personal shoppers to Dallas's elite. Using the information Gwen e-mailed the day before, Sarah created a personal store for Evie where everything was exactly the right color, size and fit for her body type. Entire outfits, complete with shoes and accessories, hung on rolling racks lining the walls.

Evie started out hesitantly, seeming unsure of style and overwhelmed by the choices. It didn't take long, though, for her inner fashionista to emerge, and soon she sorted through the racks like a pro. Haute couture welcomed her with open arms, and Evie was still going strong three hours later.

She'd even worn out Sarah, who Gwen thought never tired of shopping.

Safely ensconced on an out-of-the-way couch, she kept half an eye on Evie's "yes" pile to be sure nothing violated the brief list of fashion taboos provided by Marcus and Will and spent the time brooding. Unfortunately she couldn't find any answers or reasonable explanations for her behavior.

Sarah eventually turned Evie over to one of the Personal Shoppers with the excuse that Evie would need one in the future anyway, and tiptoed carefully through the colorful mess to Gwen's sofa.

"The child can shop." Sarah slid her feet out of their purple slingbacks and wiggled her toes in relief.

Gwen laughed. "That she can. I'm exhausted just watching."

"She's a natural. Great sense of style and an eye for what works. She'll be a real trendsetter in a couple of years."

"I'm just glad Parkline has a uniform, or else I'd be sitting here for *days*."

Sarah chuckled. "All that's really left is formal wear and she only needs one or two right now. Chris from Lingerie is on her way, so it should wind down after that. Out of curiosity, does she have a spending limit?"

Gwen watched as assistants slid Evie's purchases into giant shopping bags. "I guess not. At least not that I was told." Waving in the direction of the growing pile, she asked, "Do y'all deliver?"

"Looking at the commission Liza is about to earn off Evie, I'm sure she'll work something out."

"Thank goodness."

Sarah handed her a bottle of water. "Speaking of working out, how's everything going with the handsome-yet-infuriating Will Harrison?"

Oh, great. Exactly the conversation she didn't want to have. "About the same. Evie called him on using his BlackBerry at the table last night."

"She didn't!"

"Oh, yes, she did. In front of Marcus Heatherton."

Sarah's jaw dropped. "You must have been dying."

"That's one way to put it."

"What'd he say?"

"Marcus or Will?"

"Will, silly. Like I care about what Pillar-of-Society Marcus Heatherton thinks."

"Nothing actually. Evie's remark kind of got lost in the whole temper fit she had, so I never heard him address it."

"But after dinner, surely one of you said something."

Heat rushed to her cheeks as the image of Will leaning toward her on the couch flashed in her mind. "Um…not really…um, we were talking about, um, other things."

"Gwennie…" Sarah tucked her feet under her and leaned in. "You're blushing. What aren't you telling me?"

Her sister knew her too well. "I'm not telling you anything."

"So there is *something* to tell."

"I mean, I'm *not* not telling you anything. Or nothing. Or…you know what I mean." Flustered, she unscrewed the top of her water bottle and took a long drink.

"Did you and Will…" Sarah glanced around quickly, but the assistants had moved on and Evie and her personal shopper were still chattering away in the dressing room. "Did you two, you know?"

"No!" Gwen's ears were burning from the blush. She probably looked like an overripe tomato by now. "I barely know him, Sarah. Jeez. Get your mind out of the gutter."

"But something happened or else you wouldn't be that attractive shade of red. Will made a play, then."

"No." Lord, was that tiny voice hers? "I mean, sorta. Maybe he did?" This was embarrassing.

"Ah." Sarah got to use her all-knowing worldly-wise Big Sister Voice. "I'm going to assume there was no actual physical contact, right?"

Gwen nodded.

"But from the tone of your voice, it sounds like you wanted him to. Well? Do you, Gwennie?"

Exhausted from asking herself the same thing, Gwen gave up trying to fend off her sister's questions and gave in to the desire to unload on someone. "Sometimes. Wait, let me finish," she said as Sarah started to interrupt. "God knows the man is handsome and charming and enough to make any red-blooded woman lust after him. But developing a crush on Will would be *bad.* Bad for me. Bad for this job. Bad for my whole career, possibly."

"But you never know. Maybe he's getting a little crush on you, too."

Gwen snorted. "Not likely. I simply train the Princesses— I don't get Prince Charming."

"There's a first time for everything."

She spared another quick glance around. "We both know what happened the last time I got involved with my boss. I lost my job. I had to leave *town,* for God's sake. I'm not stupid enough to make that same mistake twice."

"No, you let David offer you up like a sacrificial lamb to save his own sorry skin and you slunk out of D.C. with your tail between your legs."

"My reputation was shot. No one would have hired me after that fiasco."

"That's an exaggeration." Sarah held up a hand to keep her

from interrupting. "It doesn't matter now. It's over and done with and you've established yourself here. You're older and wiser and you have a sterling reputation. I don't see any reason why you can't explore a possible romantic relationship with an attractive man—"

"Whom I just happen to work for?" Had Sarah lost her mind completely this time?

"This is a bit different. David was your boss. Will Harrison is your client."

"You're splitting hairs. And any way you look at it, it still leads to the same disastrous end." Gwen closed her eyes and took a deep breath. "I just need to start dating again. Got anyone in mind?"

"You mean other than Will?" she smirked.

"Sarah, *please*."

"I'll think about it. Meanwhile—"

A flash of ice-blue caught her eye and she turned. "Evie!" How long had she been standing there? She searched Evie's face for a sign she'd overhead their whispered conversation, but Evie seemed to be fully focused on twirling in front of the mirror.

Sarah shot her a look that said the conversation wasn't over, and Gwen made a mental note to screen her calls for the next few days. She had enough on her plate without adding Sarah's overromanticized matchmaking.

But Sarah was right about one thing. She wasn't the same naive girl she was five years ago. Last night's odd moment with Will could be—would *have* to be—forgotten. She'd just needed a reminder of how far she'd come.

Will knew he should be more concerned about the fact Nancy was ill and less irritated because it threw his life into disarray, but it was increasingly hard to do so when the temp sent up from HR was next to worthless. Maybe "worthless" was too harsh of a word; Nancy spoiled him with her efficiency and her ability to know what he needed without him having to spell it out. The only task the temp, Jenni, managed to complete in the last five hours was ordering flowers for Nancy. Everything else lay in various stages of completion on her desk.

He sincerely hoped Nancy got well quickly, because, damn it, he wanted his secretary back.

Now Jenni wasn't answering her intercom. This was ridiculous. Cursing, he made a list of everything that absolutely had to be done today, carried it to Nancy's desk and stuck it to the computer screen. When Jenni came back from wherever the hell she'd disappeared to, she'd have no reason not to see it.

A folder labeled "G. Sawyer" caught his eye. Why would that be on Nancy's desk? He opened it and found copies of the contract and nondisclosure agreement inside, as well as a check from his personal account for the full amount of Gwen's services. Nancy must have written the check the afternoon before but not had time to give it to him for his signature. He removed the check and left a sticky note for Nancy explaining he would deliver it personally. He placed the folder back in Nancy's in-box, and went back to his office.

It was three-thirty on a Friday afternoon. Without Nancy, much of his normal daily business had come to a complete halt, and it made zero sense to try to work on anything important. The late summer sunshine streamed through the wall of windows.

What the hell. His e-mail in-box was empty. The silence from the offices surrounding his meant most of the executive staff had left early. He should give himself a break and cut out early as well. He could take Evie and Gwen out to dinner.

Whistling, he packed up and called it a day. His receptionist stuttered as he walked by and wished her a good weekend. The security guard in the lobby checked his watch, confusion evident on his face. How long had it been since he'd left the office early?

He called home only to be informed by Mrs. Gray that Evie and Gwen weren't back from their shopping trip yet. He gave her the evening off and tried Evie on her cell phone.

"Did you have fun shopping?"

"It was amazing, Will. I found the most awesome dress for the Med Ball, and Sarah and Liza had like the entire store in my size in the dressing room and all I had to do was try stuff on."

Evie bubbled over with excitement. Something else he owed Gwen for: making Evie smile. "Sarah and Liza?"

"Sarah's Gwen's sister. She's great, but not as great as Gwen. Liza's my new personal shopper."

Personal shopper? "Remind me I want my credit card back."

"Oh, no problem. Liza set me up my own account."

Gwen laughed in the background, and Evie kept chattering away. When she paused for breath, he interrupted. "Are y'all done for the day?"

Evie relayed the question to Gwen, and he thought he heard an "Oh, definitely" before Evie replied, "I guess so."

"How about I take you to dinner tonight? I gave Mrs. Gray the night off, and maybe we could catch a movie afterward."

"Can Gwen come, too?"

"If she'd like."

Evie's voice muffled as she invited Gwen to join them for dinner and a movie. He didn't realize he was holding his breath until Evie came back on the line.

"She says yes, but not any place fancy. She didn't pack any dressy clothes."

He was oddly pleased at the way this was working out. "That will work. I'm on my way home now, so I'll see you in a little bit."

"You're on your way home *now?*" Evie sounded shocked.

"Well, yes. Is that a problem?"

"No, you just never leave work early."

She made him sound like some kind of workaholic. Maybe in her eyes he was.

Traffic was light and he made it home in record time. The doorman looked surprised to see him and asked if everything was all right. Okay, he really was working too much.

The quiet of the apartment felt unusual now, whereas in the past he'd never noticed the silence. He turned on the TV for background noise—first to the twenty-four-hours news channel, then changed his mind and scrolled through the channels for something else. He settled on a bio-documentary on John Lennon and grabbed a beer from the fridge. He tossed his tie on the coffee table before propping his feet on it, sipped his beer, and waited for Evie and Gwen to get home.

He didn't have to wait very long. Evie burst through the front door still talking a mile a minute to Gwen about something called espadrilles before interrupting herself to shout, "Will, we're home! Come see what I got!"

Hard on the heels of her words, Evie and Gwen turned the corner into the living room, weighed down by what had to be a large portion of Neiman Marcus's stock. Ricky, the doorman, followed, his arms also overflowing.

Will flashed on a memory of Evie's mother returning from marathon shopping in the early days of her marriage loaded down in much the same way. Evie must have inherited the gene from Rachel. "Did you leave anything at the store?"

"Just the stuff that needs to be altered. It won't be ready until next week." Evie was already headfirst in one of the bags, pulling out clothes and shoes for him to see.

Gwen's smile was tired as she off-loaded bags and boxes and took bags from Ricky's outstretched arms. "Thanks for saving us another trip."

"My pleasure, Miss Sawyer. Miss Evie must've really enjoyed herself today."

"I think she did." Gwen graced Ricky with a smile that had Ricky blushing behind his freckles.

"I'm glad to hear it."

"So am I," Will added, as Ricky pocketed a hefty tip and left. "But you look worn-out."

Gwen sank to the couch and toed off her shoes. "Evie is a power shopper. I'm not. I'm *never* doing that again."

"From the looks of it, she'll never need to shop again."

Gwen closed her eyes and leaned her head back. "Just wait until the new spring lines come out."

Evie continued to rifle through bags, and clothing piled up around her.

"Evie, start taking all this back to your room."

"Okay. Gwen, do you—? Never mind. I've got it. You just stay there and…and…relax." She scooped up an armload and disappeared.

Gwen opened one eye. "What was that about?"

He sat next to her. "Remorse, maybe?"

"Trust me, the shopping elite care not who they exhaust in their quest." Her eyes slid closed again, and the corners of her mouth twitched. "My sister says she has a good eye for style. She's going to be a sensation."

For the first time since he'd met her, Gwen seemed fully relaxed. Since her eyes were closed, he allowed himself to study her, his eyes roaming freely over the arch of her dark eyebrows, the curve of her cheek, and the line of her jaw. Her hair fanned behind her, the loose curls snaking along the back of the couch toward his hands. She had a beautiful, elegant profile, and he mentally traced the line down her face, over a soft neck until the chain of her necklace drew his eye to a pendant nestled at the top of gently sloping cleavage.

He had no business ogling the woman, but she intrigued him and stirred his blood in a way he hadn't felt in a long time. Unable to stop himself, he reached for the lock of hair that fell across her shoulder. He rubbed his fingers over its silkiness before tucking it gently behind her ear.

"*My* sister says you're the best. I think I might agree."

Gwen's eyes flew open at the quiet statement and a shiver slid down her neck from the touch of his fingers on her ear. She turned to meet his gaze, only to see a heat there she didn't expect.

Déjà vu. Same couch. Same desire pooling in her stomach,

same fluttery feeling in her chest. As much as she'd tried to write last night off as an aberration, she couldn't deny the repeat of sensations that rippled over her when Will's eyes lit like that and the room shrank until there seemed to only be enough oxygen for one.

Will's hand slid down her jaw until his fingers cupped her chin. Heat moved over her skin, and she wanted nothing more than to curl into his hand.

Bad idea, remember? It would be oh-so-easy to fall into Will's arms, and every nerve ending in her body screamed at her to do so, but she couldn't.

Nothing good could come of this.

Oh, yes there could, her body argued.

Will's thumb stroked the sensitive skin under her chin, causing a shiver to run over her. She followed his gaze to the rapid rise and fall of her cleavage as her breathing grew shallow, watching in horror as her nipples hardened under his stare.

It took every bit of fortitude she had to pull away.

"Will, I…I…I need to go check on Evie. Excuse me."

Coward.

Will's confused look wasn't lost on her as she fled down the hallway. Music blared from behind Evie's closed door, so Gwen didn't bother to stop and knock.

In the safety of her bedroom, she collapsed across the bed and tried to calm her rapid heartbeat. She stared at the ceiling and mentally recited her list of reasons why kissing Will would be a bad idea.

By the fourth time she made it through the complete list, she almost believed it. But once Evie was launched and she was back in her own house, she would *have* to start dating again.

She wasn't sure how long she lay there, but it seemed like only minutes later before Evie knocked at her door.

"Come in."

"Are you okay?" Evie's forehead furrowed when she saw Gwen on the bed.

"I'm fine. Just recuperating from your shopping trip. You nearly wore me out."

The furrow disappeared and Evie grinned. "Sarah warned me you were a lightweight. But it was fun, and if I haven't said 'thanks' already…"

"My pleasure, honey."

"Will sent me to tell you that he made dinner reservations, and we'll need to leave in half an hour to make it. So if you want to change or something…"

Gwen hesitated. She'd forgotten all about dinner. Considering what just happened, she should probably stay here. Better yet, she should pack and go home.

Evie picked up on her hesitation. "You are still coming, right? We're going to Milano's for pizza. I get to pick the movie, too. Please."

"Wouldn't you rather go with just Will? A little family time? You've been stuck with me all week."

"It'll be more fun if you come."

How could she say no when Evie looked so eager and hopeful? "All right. Give me a couple of minutes to freshen up."

"Cool. Will went to change, too, so we'll see you in a few."

Gwen fell back on the bed with a sigh. She was making way too much of next to nothing. She was probably no more than a blip on Will's radar—a "she's female, must flirt" kind of thing. She could control her hormones for dinner and a movie, and Evie would be there as a buffer.

Giving herself a hard mental slap to sort her brain out, she hauled herself off the bed and to the closet for something cute to wear.

CHAPTER SIX

"So HOW am I supposed to eat this? Knife and fork?" Evie eyeballed the slice of pizza with everything like she'd never seen anything like it before.

"Easy. You pick it up and take a bite."

Evie giggled. "*Finally.* Something I can eat with my fingers."

Gwen put on her best Miss Behavior voice. "But you must still eat with decorum." She winked, and Evie tore into the pizza with relish.

Will said something under his breath, and Evie erupted in another peal of giggles. He slid a piece of the pizza onto a plate and handed it to Gwen. She smiled her thanks, careful not to let her hand brush his as she took it.

So much for controlling her hormones. They'd been screaming at her when she'd run from the living room earlier, but they broke into new shrieks when she returned after changing. She'd known dinner would be a casual event and she'd heard Evie's remark about Will changing, but she hadn't been quite prepared when she walked in.

It was easier to remind herself of the distance she needed to keep from Will when he was in his suit and tie, but much harder when he appeared in a simple black T-shirt tucked in to body-hugging faded jeans. Her mouth had gone dry at the sight. He looked like the hero of some late-night movie, ready to peel the black T-shirt over his head and do something manly and sexy set to hard-rock music.

He was laughing with Evie, his dark hair falling across his forehead. When he turned that smile on her, she recited her mental list of Reasons This Would Be Bad until the flutters in her stomach calmed. And she kept repeating the reasons every time Will looked at her and started the flutters up again.

For the most part, it worked. Evie did make a good chaperone, talking nonstop and keeping the conversation in neutral areas. By the time they arrived at the restaurant, she felt she had it under control. As long as she avoided direct, extended eye contact with Will and kept a decent distance between them, she could act somewhat normal.

As she settled in to her second slice, Gwen realized—occasional shiver aside—she was enjoying herself.

They ate and talked about everything and nothing until her stomach hurt from laughing at Will's impersonations of Marcus and too much pizza. The movie theater was just down the block, and Evie suggested they walk off the monster dinner to make room for popcorn.

As Evie ran ahead to buy tickets, Will fell into step beside Gwen. They walked quietly for a moment down the tourist-lined streets of the West End. The night air was still slightly humid, but for a late summer night in Dallas, the weather couldn't have been nicer. The silence between them stretched with each step, until it changed from "companionable" to "awkward."

Searching for something to say, Gwen settled on, "Thank you for dinner."

Will nodded. "My pleasure. I'm glad you came with us." He shoved his hands into his back pockets and hunched his shoulders, a move so out of character with the man she thought she knew, she did a real double take. Will wasn't looking at her, though. His eyes were on Evie, and she got a lovely view of his strong profile.

"I guess I should apologize for earlier. I'm sorry I made you uncomfortable."

Why did he have to bring that back up? She'd been doing such a good job up until then. She took a deep breath. "Uncomfortable" would not be the word *she'd* have chosen, but she'd work with it. "Please don't worry about it. We'll just forget it, okay?"

He turned to face her, his features inscrutable, forcing her to stop walking. "Why?"

Why? "Because it will be easier for everyone if we pretend it didn't happen."

Will stepped closer to her, and she found herself eye level with the small hollow at the base of his throat. All she'd have to do is lean in…

"I mean, why were you so uncomfortable?"

"Oh." A dozen different reasons sprang to mind, but none seemed appropriate. She settled for a version of the truth. "Because I work for you, remember?"

"And?"

That wasn't enough? Maybe Will *was* the type to go fishing in the company pond. "It could also make it more difficult for me to work with Evie. You did want me to give her my full attention, correct?" Will didn't move, and every time she inhaled, the scent of him filled her. "Plus, it's hardly appropriate behavior."

"I guess I can't argue with that." Will's voice stayed bland.

You could try. No! What was she thinking?

Will stepped back and she could breathe more normally again. "Come on, Evie's waiting on us." He placed his hand on the small of her back again to steer her, and the heat made puddles of her insides.

Okay, so that went easier than expected. Case closed. Will seemed to agree with her, and as long as she kept her distance, she'd be fine. No more "almosts" and she'd get that embarrassing crush under control. She only had to hold it together for two more weeks.

Hopefully he'd have to work a lot and time would pass quickly.

Will didn't know if he should be insulted at the implication he could "just forget" the way she'd reacted to his touch and the desire he'd seen in her eyes or amused at how Gwen retreated behind that wall of politeness with some garbage about "appropriateness."

But he couldn't exactly push her any further while standing on the side of the street with Evie only a few yards away, either. He let Gwen put distance between them as she chatted with Evie and went to purchase popcorn and drinks. Evie produced the tickets to some blow 'em up thriller he'd never heard of, and he let her lead the way into the darkened theater.

Evie chose seats in the middle of the row about halfway up. When Evie sat, Gwen passed her to sit on the other side. Will flipped down the seat next to Evie and sat the vat of popcorn in her lap. As the trailers played, Evie fidgeted in her seat.

"Will, I can't see. Trade with me?"

The person in front of Evie didn't seem tall enough to block her vision, but he shrugged and switched seats. Evie handed him the popcorn and whispered, "Be sure to share with Gwen."

Evie could use some lessons in subtlety. He wondered which of her tutors could work that in to a lesson plan.

Not that he minded. His elbow brushed Gwen's on the armrest, and she pulled away with a whispered "Excuse me."

"Popcorn?"

"No, thank you." She fixed her eyes on the screen and ignored him as the movie started. Okay, so he couldn't honestly say she was ignoring him since watching the movie *was* technically what they were here to do, but she didn't look his way again.

He lost interest in the movie quickly, which was fine since he was far more interested in the woman sitting as far away from him as the small theater seat would allow. He didn't fully understand the magnetic pull of Gwen, but as he'd already discovered, it was nearly impossible to resist. His earlier resolve of not getting involved with his sister's tutor—much less a woman from outside his normal sphere—was rapidly eroding. They were both adults and the attraction was obviously mutual. As long as they kept things low-key, he couldn't think of a single good reason not to explore that mutual attraction—regardless of where it ranked on Miss Behavior's appropriateness scale.

Gwen continued to give him what he was beginning to call the Polite Treatment as they walked back to the car and during the drive home. An outsider would never surmise anything was wrong, and at no point could he say she was anything other than the perfect guest. She was just so stinking *polite,* and he knew it was a complete act.

Back at the apartment, he opened the door and held it for Evie and Gwen. Evie took a mere two steps inside before she stretched her arms over her head and yawned loudly.

"I'm pooped and going to bed. See you in the morning. G'nite, Will. G'nite, Gwen."

The kid was a terrible actress. But she was in her room with the door closed before her words quit echoing, and he was left alone with Gwen for the second time that day.

"I'm pretty beat myself," Gwen said a bit too brightly. "I think I'll head on to bed, too. Thank yo—"

He interrupted her, knowing full well how interrupting hovered close to the top of Gwen's list of pet peeves, but there was really no avoiding it. He wasn't going to let her retreat behind closed doors just yet. "There are a couple of things we still need to clear up."

"Really? What do you…" She trailed off as he closed the slight distance between them, and she took two small steps backward only to find her back against the foyer wall. Her eyes flashed as he took advantage of her position and moved within inches of her body.

Reaching out, he captured the errant lock of hair that draped across her shoulder again. Twisting it around his finger, he played with the silky strand until her breathing became shallow, and she asked, "*What,* Will?"

"First, business and pleasure are two totally separate situations. I'm not one to confuse the two, and I'm surely not going to deny myself one because of the other. I hired you to work with Evie. This—" he released her hair, only to move his hand to the elegant column of her neck, pleased to feel the pulse thumping wildly there "—has nothing to do with that."

Gwen's eyes widened as his other hand slid up her neck to cradle her jaw. She leaned in toward him, and he felt his own heartbeat accelerate.

"Secondly, Miss Behavior, I don't give a damn about what's appropriate."

Oh. *My.* Gwen's thoughts scrambled, and her libido woke with a mighty cheer. Will's face hovered inches from hers, and for the first time in a long time, she didn't give a damn about appropriateness, either.

Yes, you do, her conscience argued, but it was a token protest rapidly smothered by the need that had been simmering all evening and burst to life at the touch of his fingers on her skin.

She lifted her hand to his chest, where his heart thumped heavily with excitement. It slid, seemingly of its own accord, up over soft black cotton until she found the warm skin at his collar. Will's breath hissed as her fingers moved around strong muscles to his nape and slid up to tangle in his silky hair. *Just one little kiss, that's all...*

That slight pressure seemed to be all the permission he needed, and his mouth closed on hers. A lifetime of civility hadn't prepared her for the raw power of his kiss or the force of sensations that ripped through her. Heat. Hunger. Desire.

His tongue slipped across hers, tasting and tempting, and demanding a response, as lightning bolted down her spine and lit her on fire. Her hand tightened in his hair, holding him to her as she melted from the contact.

The man can kiss, she thought, before he trailed scorching kisses along her jaw to the soft spot at the base of her ear. All remaining rational thought fled when Will nipped the sensitive skin with strong teeth, and she gave over to the purely carnal thrill of his touch.

And, oh, oh, oh…his touch. Will's hands moved from her neck, massaging circles down the tense muscles of her back, to the indentation of her waist, where his fingers splayed for a momentary squeeze before pulling her body into complete contact with his.

Hard thighs. Powerful chest. Strong arms holding her against him. She rose on tiptoe, aligning her hips with the straining bulge in his jeans. Will groaned, his hand moving to the small of her back to hold her in place. Unadulterated want slammed into her, leaving her reeling on wobbly legs.

"Will," she whispered against his lips.

He broke the kiss, his breath coming in short pants and looked down at her with heavy-lidded eyes. A heartbeat later, he set her away from him, keeping his hands on her hips to steady her.

"I know." He exhaled and dropped his forehead to hers. "I got a bit carried away there."

Coherent thought eluded her. What? What was he talking about? *Why* was he talking? Her foggy brain wouldn't clear and she tried to make sense of his words. Will held her hand loosely as he led her down the long hallway to her bedroom door.

Twining his fingers in hers, he kissed her knuckles before brushing his lips gently across her mouth. "Good night, Gwen. See you in the morning."

Good night? What? No! Clarity arrived moments too late as she watched Will disappear into his bedroom at the end of the hall.

No, no, no! Damn it! Needy nerve cells screamed at her to call him back, to bang on his door and demand he continue where he left off. Her skin tingled with electrical afterglow and she throbbed in sync with her heartbeat. She took a step toward Will's closed door.

Thankfully her sanity chose that moment to return. What on earth was she doing? Even worse, what had she done? Making out with Will Harrison in the hallway while his teenage sister was just footsteps away? Not to mention the whole "it would be bad to sleep with your boss" thing. She'd lost what was left of her cotton-picking mind with that one kiss.

One mind-blowing, toe-curling, too-good-to-be-real kiss.

She retreated to her bedroom and closed the door softly behind her. Kicking off her shoes, she left them where they landed and padded across the carpet to the cool marble tiles of the adjoining bath. Cold water splashed on her face helped bring her back to reality, and a sigh-by-sigh replay of what just happened flashed across her mind in Technicolor.

She closed her eyes and groaned. She'd practically climbed him like a tree. But, oh, what a fine tree he was, all heat and hardness….

Gwen forced her eyes open, banishing the visual, only to grimace at her reflection in the mirror. Her hair stood at crazy angles, and a vague memory of his hands tangling in it and massaging her scalp stirred. A flush rode high on her cheekbones. Her mouth looked swollen. Water droplets glistened at her temples, and she remembered how Will had kissed her there, too.

She could hear water running in the bathroom next to hers. Will was in the shower. That was all her libido needed to roar back to life—the thought of Will warm and slick and soapy….

This had to stop. She visualized the place setting for a

seven-course formal dinner that included a fish course and a cheese course. Keeping that image firmly in the front of her mind, she named each piece of the setting by course, hoping it would be unsexy enough to banish Will's kisses from her immediate memory. Gwen grabbed her brush from the countertop and attacked the tangles in her hair.

"Bread plate, butter knife, salad fork…" Six courses later, she'd managed to brush her hair and teeth and change into her pajamas without too much fantasizing. She turned off the lights and crawled under the covers. In the dark, fish forks weren't much of a distraction, and she returned to her list of Reasons This Would Be Bad and focused intently on reason number one: potential career suicide. Again.

Things had started out exciting with David, too—okay, he wasn't nearly as tantalizing as Will, but at twenty-two, she'd been much more naive and David had seemed so perfect. Handsome, successful, charming. As the top student in her class, she'd scored the most coveted of all possible internships: working for the most prestigious lobby group in D.C. When David offered her the chance to work on a plum project, she'd jumped at the opportunity, even if it did mean spending long hours after five in the close confines of his office—just the two of them. She'd fallen hard, and thought David felt the same, at least until *his* boss found them in a compromising position in the supply closet, and she'd become a Washington cliché in seconds flat. She'd found out then exactly how much David "loved" her. He managed to save *his* career by painting her as a grasping opportunist trying to sleep her way into a great job, and when the project went to hell days later, he let her take the fall for that as well—even though the blame should have landed solely at his feet. She'd been too heartbroken to fight back—even if she'd known how—and between the gossip about her personal life and the speculation of how she managed to flub such an important project, her job leads dried up.

Her broken heart had mended quickly thanks to the anger at being used, but it had taken a lot longer to get over the shame of it, and the five years she'd spent in Dallas building a spotless reputation had given her new perspective on the whole sordid affair. She knew better now.

Then *why* had she ended up in Will's arms, practically begging him to take her off to bed with him? She needed to be careful. Even if her heart could take another hit, her career certainly couldn't.

Sleep was a long time coming.

Cold showers always worked like magic in movies and books. But the characters in movies and books obviously hadn't been kissing Gwen, because the longest, coldest shower in the universe hadn't removed the lingering imprint of Gwen's body from his or chased away the haunting scent of her skin.

Will toweled off, scrubbing at the chill bumps on his skin, and tried to think of something other than the feel of Gwen's tongue sliding over his like a promise.

The fact he'd practically mauled her in the hallway popped to mind, followed closely by the realization that he'd have no one to blame but himself if Gwen packed up her tea set and moved out first thing in the morning. He hadn't intended for the kiss to go that far, that quickly. He just hadn't been prepared for the desire that had slammed into him at the taste of her.

Still…if she hadn't brought him to his senses when she did, he'd still be happily pawing her in his foyer. Or maybe they'd have made it as far as his room by now.

Gwen felt the attraction between them. That much he knew. She'd been an active and willing participant in that kiss, even if she was probably flogging herself with the inappropriateness of it by now.

Provided Gwen didn't hightail it out of here tomorrow at the crack of dawn, he'd start changing her mind about what constituted "appropriate."

That should prove interesting.

His body still wanted to knock on Miss Behavior's door and, well, *misbehave*, but it was under control enough for him to crawl under the covers and contemplate his next move instead. It wasn't often that Fate delivered an interesting, attractive woman to his door like a belated birthday present, and he wasn't going to waste the opportunity.

Vague notions he should use the late-night quiet to break out his laptop and work for a while intruded briefly, but, for once, he was completely uninterested in HarCorp and business problems. He chuckled. There was a first time for everything.

His plans for Gwen were *much* more interesting to think about. In no time at all, he found himself in need of another cold shower.

CHAPTER SEVEN

GOING back to her regular life in two weeks was going to suck. Gwen sat beside the rooftop pool of Will's condo building— a private pool only for use by the residents of the top three floors—and tried to read and relax.

A striped cabana shaded her from the sun, and as she leaned back against matching pillows with a cold drink, she half expected a cabana boy to show up with a bottle of suntan oil and offer to rub some on her.

Evie lay on her stomach in the sun beside the cabana, her feet moving slightly in rhythm to the music on her iPod as she conjugated a series of irregular French verbs. A Geometry text topped a pile of books next to her. Yesterday's shopping, dinner, and movie extravaganza must have put her behind on her homework. One of the etiquette books stuck out at an awkward angle from her pile as well; a ribboned bookmark indicated Evie was about halfway finished.

Fluffy white clouds spotted an otherwise clear blue sky, and a breeze fluttered the pages of the book in her lap. By all definitions, it was a perfect day. She would be relaxed and lost in her book by now if not for the constant sound of splashes coming from the pool.

The noise wasn't what was disturbing her. The *cause* of the splashes was. If she lifted her eyes from her book she wasn't actually reading, she'd see the pool and the powerful body making lap after lap. Will moved through the water like a pro, each stroke strong and sure. The sight of the water sliding over his body sent her mind back to the thought of Will in the shower the night before, which immediately sent her thoughts back to the kiss in the foyer.

Not that she needed much help remembering that kiss. The feel of Will was branded into her skin. She could still taste him on her lips. What little sleep she'd managed last night had only allowed her mind to carry that kiss to erotic extremes in her dreams.

After such a restless night, she crawled out of bed early to head to Sarah's house for coffee and a visit with Letitia. The spoiled cat curled into her lap purring and refused to move, keeping her pinned in the chair and under her sister's inquisition much longer than comfortable. *How* Sarah had been able to tell Gwen had been thoroughly kissed, she'd never know, but Sarah wouldn't rest until every last embarrassing detail was dissected to her satisfaction.

Yet Gwen still didn't have any concrete answers—not for why she'd kissed Will, not for what she wanted to happen next, nothing. After two hours and two pots of coffee, she'd finally been able to escape her sister—who really wasn't helping the situation *at all*—and headed back to what was beginning to feel like the lion's den.

Gwen hadn't thought to ask about how Evie and Will spent their weekends, and she'd returned to the condo to find them headed to the pool. Against her better judgment, she allowed them to convince her to join them. She regretted the decision instantly after Will stripped down to nothing but a pair of black swim trunks. Thankfully her sunglasses hid the unladylike and unflattering way her eyes had to have bugged at the sight of all that bronze skin and hard muscle. She'd run to the safety of the cabana immediately, very glad when Will dove straight into the water instead of taking the other lounge chair.

Now Evie was engrossed with homework, and she was having a hard time pulling her eyes away from Will.

It's rude to stare. But next to impossible not to, she told herself. She lost count of how many laps he completed long ago, but he showed no signs of tiring. That explained the tan. And the shoulders. And the chest… She reached for her water bottle, rolling it across the heated skin of her neck and chest before taking a long drink to try to lower her temperature. With a sigh, she tried to concentrate on the words in her book, thankful neither Evie nor Will were paying her any attention at all.

Water splashed at her feet, and she looked up to see Will, all wet and wonderful, standing in the shallow end of the pool, ready to send another stream of water at Evie.

"Hey!" Evie shouted, "You're getting my homework all wet."

"Aren't you two coming in?" Water dripped from his dark hair onto his shoulders before joining the rivulets running down his chest and over the muscles of his stomach. *Her* stomach contracted at the sight.

Mercy. The man should be on billboards.

Evie closed her notebook and took a running dive into the deep end. As graceful in the water as her brother—if not more so—she swam the length of the pool and surfaced not far from Will.

Cupping her hand, Evie expertly sent a spray of water straight into Will's face. He shook it off, sending droplets in all directions.

"Oh, big mistake, squirt."

Evie squealed as Will pelted her with sheets of water until she begged for mercy. For Gwen, it was a much-needed distraction from her brooding and drooling over Will. When he stopped, Evie sent one last spray his way, then swam quickly to Gwen's side of the pool.

Will's arm pulled back, ready to continue.

"Better not, Will. You'll get Gwen all wet."

Gwen laughed. "Oh, no, don't come running to me for protection. You're on your own, kiddo." She made a show of wrapping her book in a towel and placing it out of immediate water damage.

"Traitor," Evie wailed before she disappeared under a wall of water that drenched Gwen as well.

The cold water took her breath away. She pushed her sopping bangs out of her eyes to see a completely unrepentant Will grinning at her.

Something lightened inside of her chest, and she grabbed the feeling and the moment with both hands.

"Oh, you are so dead meat, Will Harrison. Come on, Evie."

That was all the warning he got before she jumped feet-first into the pool and joined Evie in sending as much water at Will as humanly possible.

She wasn't as good at it as Will and Evie, but at least two-against-one helped even the odds a bit. Will fought back, using both arms and hands to keep the water flying as he moved in her direction and backed her up against the pool wall, leaving her helpless under the constant fall of water.

Evie, that little traitor, switched allegiances and joined Will in dousing her.

She needed to get off the wall and back in the open. Gwen calculated her move, waited for the right second, then slid quickly to her left, planning to go under, push off the wall and slip quickly between them.

No such luck. Will moved at just the wrong—or possibly right—moment, and her push off the wall sent her barreling straight into him. Those strong arms locked around her and pulled her to the surface, keeping her trapped against his chest.

His wet, hard, stuff-of-fantasies *bare* chest.

Gwen's shout of outrage died in her throat as the bare skin of her back burned where it pressed against his. She gasped instead. Every memory of last night's kiss and the fantasies it inspired flashed across her mind.

"You got her, Will!"

"Indeed I do." He lowered his voice and dropped his head closer to her ear. "Now what should I do with you?"

She shivered as much from the whisper of breath across her ear as from his words. Will answered her shiver with a squeeze that pressed her more firmly against him. Every inch of her—from shoulders to ankles—sizzled at the contact. The seconds stretched out as she reveled in the sensation. But the hard flesh nestling right above the swell of her bottom brought her attention rocketing back to his whispered question.

"I call for a t-truce."

Will chuckled in her ear and whispered, "Coward." But he did release her, and she sank into the cool water, allowing it to balm her burning skin. With a knowing wink in her direction that only scrambled her thoughts more, Will swam away to the other side of the pool.

Gwen climbed the ladder on trembling legs and retreated to the relative safety of the cabana. She would not take the bait of being called a coward, but she wasn't going to run and hide in her room, either. She placed her sunglasses firmly in front of her eyes, buried her nose in her book and tried to calm her rapid breathing.

Evie produced a Frisbee, and she and Will began a noisy game of catch, giving her a much-needed opportunity to mentally regroup.

Sarah had been brutally direct this morning with her analysis of the situation. *"Sounds to me like the attraction is mutual."*

Okay, so maybe it was. She couldn't deny or ignore Will's attraction to her, and she knew for damn certain she wasn't immune to him. Sarah had listened to the full list of Reasons This Would Be Bad, but countered with romanticized possibilities that would ease any worst-case scenarios.

There was no romanticizing or outthinking the biggest Bad Reason, however, and that Reason was rapidly moving to the top of her list.

And that Reason would be how much she liked Will. *Really*

liked Will. Irritating BlackBerry, bouts of overbearing arrogance and all, she'd finally found a man she liked to talk to. One who could surprise her and make her laugh at the strangest things. Everything she thought she knew about him had proved false; instead she'd found a handsome, charming, funny guy who was smart and successful and cared about his little sister.

She, thanks to the papers and her debs, knew a lot about his dating history. He wasn't exactly a playboy, but he did play the field one socialite at a time. That, coupled with what she knew about Will's workaholic tendencies and bolstered by some casual comments dropped by Evie, made *liking* Will a danger. Maybe Will wasn't looking for anything permanent, but could she enjoy what he did have to offer? It would be one fabulous ride—while it lasted. Could Sarah be right and the Worst-Case Scenarios actually be fixable? Could her heart and her ego take the hit if it didn't work out?

Evie, though, was still a sticking point. She didn't want Evie to get hurt. Had Will even given thought how his serial-dating technique might affect a fifteen-year-old?

And could she handle being the next installment in that serial? She remembered the feel of Will's skin against hers and the taste of him under her lips. The gooseflesh that rose on her arms answered part of the question: her body was more than willing to give it a shot.

"Gwen?"

Gwen snapped out of her reverie to find Evie and Will standing in front of her with identical puzzled expressions. Evie had a sarong tied around her slim hips, and Will had a towel slung over his shoulders. Her eyes followed the thin line of hair down to where it disappeared into the waistband of his trunks, and her mouth went dry.

Oh, yeah, her body was more than willing.

"Book not any good?" Evie asked.

"Excuse me?" She tore her eyes from Will's abs and tried

to focus. Both of them were merely damp, meaning they'd been out of the pool for a while.

"You're not reading it. You're staring at it."

"You seemed to be pretty far away," Will added.

She looked at the book in her hands. "Oh. Yeah. Um…" She fumbled. "I was dozing a bit there. I didn't sleep well last night."

Will's eyebrow cocked up and she realized where he'd gone with her statement. *Ugh.*

Evie, though, accepted her statement at face value. "Are you hungry, then? We're going to order some take-out."

"Sure."

Evie went for the elevator while Gwen packed up her things, very aware Will was watching her.

"You were thinking pretty hard there. Come to any conclusions?"

Good Lord, was she that easy to read? Or maybe he wasn't talking about *that.* She could have easily been thinking about a number of different problems in her life. Even the strictest tenets of etiquette didn't require her to give him a complete answer, so she settled for one that would give him something to think about.

If he'd been thinking in *that* direction.

"Maybe I did."

Since the day he'd brought Evie home, he'd never wished her gone. Not once. He may have briefly considered boarding school for her, but that was because he didn't feel like a suitable person to raise a teenager, not because of her. She had her moments when he could cheerfully strangle her, but he wasn't too proud to admit he adored the kid.

So he freely embraced the guilt that prodded at him when he wished Evie somewhere else tonight. Not *gone,* just not here in the room with him and Gwen. Her room would work just fine, but at nine on a Saturday night, he had no good reason to suggest she go there.

Even if he could come up with a good reason, he was hesitant to do so. Evie was having such a good time. So was he. Even Gwen had eventually relaxed and seemed to be enjoying herself. Take-out sandwiches and DVD movies, followed by Chinese take-out and now a game of Monopoly with no end in sight. He hadn't been near his BlackBerry all day, and the upcoming meeting with the Japanese seemed a long way away. It had easily been the best Saturday he'd had in ages, and as soon as Evie went to bed, it was going to get a lot better. That much he was sure of.

Gwen might try to hide behind that Miss Behavior wall of appropriate politeness, but he knew it was starting to crumble. Last night's kiss, the way her eyes had caressed him all day, the way he'd felt her shiver with desire against him in the pool today…the next step was inevitable. He knew it, and he was damn sure she knew it too.

So as much as he'd like to investigate that inevitability right this second, he could be patient and bide his time. He was content for the moment to relax against the sofa and nurse his beer while his sister beat them soundly at Monopoly.

Gwen sat across the game board from him, also on the floor, her bare feet with their bright red toes tucked underneath her. After her shower, she'd dressed in a pair of cutoffs and a white T-shirt, and her hair fell loose around her face. Without makeup, she looked even younger, and as she paid Evie for landing on Boardwalk, he wondered how old she was. At that moment, he realized he didn't know all that much about her.

Evie, of course, probably knew Gwen's entire life story by now; too bad he couldn't ask her. He settled for something simple and innocuous.

"So, Gwen, how did you come to be Miss Behavior?"

Gwen cocked her head, seemingly surprised at the question. "Well, that's kind of a long story."

He looked over at Evie, who was busy counting her piles of money with glee. "I think we have time while Miss Moneybags plays in her ill-gotten gains."

Evie stuck her tongue out at him. "You're just a sore loser. I'm going for another soda. Anyone want anything?"

Gwen shook her head, then settled back against a chair. "Well, I moved to Dallas five years ago after Sarah got her job at Neiman Marcus. I'd finished protocol training in D.C., done an internship and needed to land somewhere. I don't really have a hometown because we moved so much, and since my folks mentioned eventually retiring in Texas, this seemed like a good choice."

"I knew you didn't sound native."

"Nope. But my dad grew up in Houston, does that count?"

He nodded. "So how'd you end up on a Web site?"

She chuckled. "Accidentally, I assure you. I never planned to do anything with teenagers. But when I got to Dallas, I needed a job. I started working with a friend of mine who did some deb training on the side, and it worked out pretty well. I made a name for myself doing that without really meaning to. 'Miss Behavior' was a nickname my deb class gave me a few years ago, and when one of those debs started the TeenSpace site, she called and asked if I wanted to be one of the columnists. The rest is history."

"Sounds like you fell into the right job, though."

"Maybe. But I can't be Miss Behavior forever."

"Sarah says Gwen wants to ditch the debs and go back to working with grown-ups." Evie sat back in her place and eyeballed the stacks of money.

"Grown-ups?"

"Sarah needs to keep her mouth shut," Gwen muttered.

"Sarah says Gwen's going to bigger and better things one day, but she needs the debs right now because that's who's paying her rent," Evie continued.

That reminded him. Her check was still in his briefcase.

"Thank you, Evie. That's quite enough."

Gwen's carefully clipped tone made him laugh silently. He loved to watch Gwen wrap herself in politeness. Too bad he couldn't prod her more often.

"Gwen speaks Japanese, you know."

"Ev-ie!" Gwen looked ill at ease, but he didn't know why.

"Well, you do. I didn't know it was some kind of secret," Evie grumbled.

"You're right. It's not a secret." Gwen turned to him. "I'm not completely fluent, but I get by. I also speak German and a little French. No," she added as Evie perked up and opened her mouth to say something. "I won't conjugate those verbs for you. Madame Louise expects you to know them by Monday. Have you finished yet?"

Someone else might not have noticed the way Gwen subtly moved the topic away from herself, but Will did. And though he was more curious than ever to know more about her, he respected her desire for privacy—for the moment at least. Maybe it was some kind of lesson meant to teach Evie about polite conversation, and he shouldn't undermine Gwen's work to appease his own interest.

But he could use some help with his own Japanese lessons. Maybe Gwen would be willing to teach him a few phrases. The thought of private lessons with Gwen led him right back to his original wish that Evie would go to bed.

As if she'd read his mind, Evie stretched, looked at the game board pointedly and said, "If you guys will concede defeat, I'll go work on some French before I go to bed. I'm pooped."

Gwen's eyebrows went up as she glanced at the clock. It was still early, but he certainly wasn't going to argue with Evie's plan. It sounded great to him.

Once Evie left, Gwen began tidying up the game pieces. Her teeth worried her lower lip, and he wondered what she was thinking.

"Where does this go?" She indicated the box.

"Beats me. I didn't even know we owned the game." He took another long drink of his beer as Gwen rose up on her knees to place the game on the glass-topped coffee table and reached for her own glass.

She settled back in her original seat on the floor, her back against the chair and her legs stretched out in front of her. Silence stretched between them and without Evie in the room, the air became charged with electricity.

Only a few feet separated them, and he closed the distance easily, watching Gwen's eyes widen, then darken with unmistakable interest.

Will ran his hand down the silky skin of her arm and laced his fingers with hers. She didn't resist as he tugged her gently toward him, and when her pink tongue darted out to moisten her lips, what little blood was still circulating freely rushed to heat his skin.

Gwen cleared her throat. "Today was a great day."

He dipped his head to taste the soft skin on her neck and felt her shiver in response. "It's not over yet, you know."

She'd known this was going to happen. Her day of brooding may not have provided many answers, and she still wasn't sure this was the wisest course of action, but the tension inside her had her stretched to the breaking point. Will hadn't touched her since that moment in the pool, but the long, lazy looks that traveled over her as strongly as a physical caress had kept her on edge all afternoon.

She had two choices: turn tail and run or seize the moment. While retreat was the safer, far more rational choice, she'd lost the battle with her rational brain hours ago. She could be careful, try to safeguard her heart and her business, but she wasn't going to pass on what could be the most amazing man who'd ever crossed her path. Years of doing the prudent thing, of always weighing the benefits and minimizing the risks, hadn't netted her much beyond a job that didn't satisfy her and an existence that suddenly seemed rather blah and bland.

The sensation of Will's lips on her neck was far from bland, and she tilted her head back to provide him greater access.

Heat rippled over her as his mouth traveled over her jaw and captured her lips.

Oh, yes. This was definitely worth the risk.

Gwen eagerly fitted her body against his, loving the feel of him, while his kiss wreaked havoc on her senses. She twined her arms around his neck, allowing her fingers to slide across the taut cords of muscles, and held on while the sensations tried to sweep her away.

She wanted to be closer, to feel more of him, to taste more of him. She pulled her mouth from his, gasping for air, and moved her lips to the same spot on his neck he'd found on her moments earlier.

She was rewarded with a hiss of pleasure as her tongue snaked out to taste his skin, and the hand that had been massaging her back in rhythm to his kiss moved down to her hip in a heat-filled caress.

Turning more fully toward him, Gwen slid her thigh over his, trying to get closer to the heat she craved. Will responded by capturing her mouth in another searing kiss, latching his hands around her hips, and lifting her until she straddled his legs.

Oh, *yesss*, she thought, as his hands locked over her buttocks and snugged her knees up next to his hips. Her new position gave her easy access to run her hands over the defined contours of his chest, over those wide shoulders, until she could bury her hands in his hair and hold his mouth against hers.

A growl of desire rumbled in Will's throat as his tongue mated wildly with hers. She gasped as his hand cupped her breast, his thumb dragging soft cotton over her distended nipple, and she arched back, allowing him greater access.

Will nuzzled her, and she cursed the T-shirt keeping his mouth from her skin. Every nerve ending screamed for his touch, and her body shook as pure want fired her blood. She wanted to feel his skin against hers, to revel in the magic his fingers worked on her, to let him soothe the ache growing deep inside her.

But not here. Sane thought clawed its way through her be-fuddled mind.

As if reading her mind, Will cupped his hands under her thighs and surged to his knees. "Not here. Evie might—"

She nodded, but he didn't release his hold on her.

"Hang on."

It took a second for Gwen to realize he meant that liter-ally. Will got to his feet, and she clung to him like a vine on a tree as he padded quickly down the long hallway, past Evie's closed door and into the master suite at the far end.

Will barely paused as he entered, simply nudging the door closed with his shoulder before crossing what seemed like a huge expanse to deposit her on her feet next to the most luxu-rious bed she'd ever seen.

This is your last chance to back out, her conscience re-minded her. She quickly stomped it back down. She wasn't going to worry about what might happen tomorrow—or the day after that. She could simply enjoy Will for the time she had him, and she'd have to trust she'd be able to make every-thing else work out.

That was her last fully lucid thought, as Will grabbed the hem of her shirt to pull it over her head. He thumbed the clasp of her bra open, tossing it to the floor with her shirt. Her shorts and panties quickly followed, and she stood naked in the half-light of the room.

Her breath came in short pants as his hungry eyes devoured her, and his fingers reached out to stroke across the slope of her breasts.

"Beautiful."

Emboldened, Gwen reached for the hem of his shirt and, with his help, it joined her clothes on the floor. She echoed his action, her fingers threading through the crisp hairs on his chest.

"I agree."

Will groaned as she touched him, the pads of her fingers finding his flat nipples and stroking over them. When she leaned forward to touch her tongue against one, he shuddered and grasped her shoulders.

Then she was on the bed, soft, cool sheets under her and the hard heat of Will covering her. *This* was heaven on earth, and she was beyond glad she hadn't talked herself out of experiencing it.

Those long, lean muscles bunched under her fingers as she traced them, memorizing their pull and play under the hot skin against hers. Shadows hid Will's face as he moved slowly down her body, making each touch of his tongue to her over-sensitized flesh an erotic surprise. In a daze, she closed her eyes and let the sensations ripple over her body unfettered as Will's hands slid over the muscles in her legs and his lips followed.

Strong teeth grazed the sensitive skin of her thigh, bringing her focus sharply back as Will draped that thigh across his shoulder and cupped her hips in his hands. One last feather-light kiss was all the warning she had before his mouth fastened on her and fire ignited in her veins.

She was mindless and shaking with need when Will finally settled between her thighs and slid into her in one smooth stroke. A hiss of pleasure escaped her as he settled into rhythm, one large hand resting on her hip to hold her in place as his body moved against hers.

Will caught her shout of pleasure in his mouth as she reached her climax, and moments later, he gave it back to her as he reached his. He relaxed on top of her, burying his face in her neck, and she could feel the pounding of his heart against her chest. Heart racing, breath coming in short gasps, she closed her eyes to enjoy the feel of his weight on her as she rubbed gentle circles on his shoulders.

Will finally lifted his head and kissed her softly before resting his forehead against hers.

"Can you breathe?"

She opened her eyes to see him staring at her, a bemused

look on his face. Actual speech was out of the question for the moment, so she nodded.

"Good. 'Cause I may never move from this spot."

Warmth pooled in her chest before she could remind herself not to read too much into his words. But she relished them anyway and savored the afterglow of the moment.

When Will's breathing finally evened out, he rolled to his back and snuggled her against his side. His hands traced lazy circles over her arms and back and she relaxed into a delicious haze.

"Gwen?"

"Hmm?"

"You're not falling asleep, are you?"

Through her languor, she managed to crack one eye. Will's half smile and hooded eyes immediately chased her laziness away. "Nope."

The smile broadened briefly before his lips captured hers again and he pulled her atop him.

CHAPTER EIGHT

GWEN smeared aloe gel over the sunburn coloring her nose and cheeks a bright red. Looked like her ears needed some, too. The burn didn't hurt—yet—but it would before the night was out. She knew better than to hope it would fade to a tan; her fair skin only burned and peeled. Tanning was for people with better genetic luck.

From the other room, she heard her sister's ring tone for the third time in the last hour. Gwen ignored it as she examined the coloring on her neck and arms in the bathroom mirror. Sarah would just have to wait. She'd know something was up the second she heard Gwen's voice, and Gwen didn't feel like deconstructing the last twenty-four hours with her sister at the moment.

Of course, that would assume *she* knew what to make of the last twenty-four hours. Which she didn't. Not by a long shot.

She'd slept late this morning, waking only when Evie returned from swimming and pounded on her door with "Gwen! Are you alive?"

Gwen had a vague recollection of Will walking her to her own room in the wee hours of the morning. Exhausted and limp-limbed from Will's lovemaking, she'd crawled under the covers and slept like the dead. Or at least like the dead with very erotic dreams.

As she forced herself out of bed and crawled into the shower, she'd worried about facing Will in the light of day, worried about how she should act and what she could say. She worried about Evie figuring out how they'd spent the night before.

But her worrying had been for nothing. Will was friendly, but not overly flirtatious, and Evie, as always, made an excellent buffer. Her chatter made awkward silences impossible, and Gwen surprised herself at the ease she felt these days around both Harrisons.

So when Will handed her a cup of coffee and asked, "Do you like the Rangers?" she answered honestly and without thinking.

"I don't really know much about baseball."

Both Will and Evie gaped at her in shock. Will, it seemed, was a huge fan, and had converted Evie. Today would be Evie's first live game, and Gwen found herself dragged along as both of them tried to indoctrinate her to the sport.

She'd spent the afternoon at a Rangers game—just not in the HarCorp skybox as she'd assumed. Oh, no. Evie's first American baseball game had to be spent in the stands, under the searing July sun, so she could get the full experience— hot dogs, popcorn and a huge foam finger to wave.

And sunburned nose notwithstanding, Gwen had enjoyed it as much as Evie—although for slightly different reasons. She might not be a baseball fan after today, but...

Gwen stared at the phone as it rang, debating how much longer she could ignore it and how many more times Sarah would try to call.

"Sorry, Sarah," she muttered as she turned the phone off. She could call her tomorrow, when Sarah would be at work and have less time for analyzing Gwen's life.

Thirsty, Gwen went to the kitchen to get a drink. While she was there, she added sunscreen to the running list Mrs. Gray kept in the pantry. Then, out of curiosity, she peeked into the living room. Will and Evie sat on opposite ends of the couch, both of them tapping away at their laptops.

Well, everyone defines family time differently, I guess.

She should probably boot up her laptop and work some, too. Instead she thought about the massive tub in her bathroom. Just what she needed.

Gwen hit Play on the CD player and sank into the hot water with a sigh. She stayed there, letting the music hypnotize her while she tried to make sense of the wild turn her life had just taken.

Don't overanalyze. Don't overthink. Just take it one day at a time. She'd made her choice, and while she didn't regret it in the least—far from it—she didn't know what, if anything, came next.

She let her thoughts wander from the practical to the fantastical—and even through the possible repercussions—until the water turned too cold for comfort. She was rubbing lotion on her legs when she heard a soft tap at her door.

Slipping into her fuzzy robe, she glanced at the clock. Ten-thirty. How long had she been in the tub?

She opened the door, expecting to see Evie. Instead Will leaned against the frame. Her heartbeat accelerated as he grinned at her. A quick glance down the hall confirmed that Evie's door was closed.

"I need to talk to you about Evie."

Oh. So it was business he was here for, not pleasure. She tamped down the niggles of disappointment as she tugged on her belt, tightening it, and adjusted the collar of her robe. "Is everything all right?"

"Everything's fine. I just thought you should know Evie went to bed forty-five minutes ago. She has an early tennis lesson tomorrow." Will's hand toyed with the collar of her robe while he spoke. She wished she'd thought to bring a nicer one. This one had been with her since college. Yes, it was comfortable, but it fit like a comfy potato sack and the collar he toyed with was frayed at the edges. Not exactly the evening attire she wanted to be caught wearing by Will. The embroidered cats frolicking along the cuffs and collar didn't help the look, either.

Slightly confused and embarrassed, she prompted him. "And...?"

"And this." His hand closed around one of the frayed kitties on her collar and pulled her close until she pressed against his chest. Then his mouth closed on hers in a searing kiss.

That kiss brought every erotic sensation from last night back to the surface in amazing, gasping detail, showing her how faulty her powers of recollection really were.

In one swift movement, Will had them fully inside her room, and her back was against the door as Will loosened the sash and her robe fell open. She heard Will murmur his appreciation at finding nothing underneath, his words muffled against her skin as he sank to his knees, kissing a path down her torso as he went.

Gwen's knees buckled, her fingers first grasping his shoulders for support as Will tasted her, then scoring him with her nails as his tongue quickly sent her over the edge.

Holding her steady as the ripples ran through her, Will stood and kissed her deeply. Behind her, she heard the lock click into place.

"Now come to bed."

Gwen woke the next morning in a very good mood, but no one was around to share it. Evie had gone to her tennis lesson earlier, Will always left for work around seven-thirty and Mrs. Gray was walking out the door with a pile of what looked like dry cleaning under her arm just as Gwen emerged from her room.

"Good morning, Miss Gwen. I've left you some coffee and rolls in the kitchen. I'm off to get more groceries—Miss Evie seems to have cleaned out the cupboards over the weekend. Can I get you anything? Do you need anything while I'm out?"

"No, but thanks." She did need a couple of things, but Gwen couldn't get used to the idea of Mrs. Gray doing it for her. Not that she should. Unless Letitia could be trained to shop, she'd be doing for herself again anyway in another ten days. This afternoon, while Evie was with her tutors, she'd run her own errands.

The morning edition of the *Tribune* sat on the marble countertop next to the coffeepot, along with the Monday edition of *Dallas Lifestyles*. Normally she'd take the time to flip through both over coffee, but she'd slept so late she really needed to get some work accomplished first.

Gwen poured herself a cup of the fragrant coffee blend Will preferred, grabbed a still-warm cinnamon roll and went back to her room to get dressed.

The coffee cleared her brain of residual sleepiness, and by the time she pulled on a pair of jeans and a T-shirt, she was fully awake. She caught herself humming as she pulled her hair up into a ponytail. Her amazingly good mood this morning had to be a residual effect of last night.

Ahh, last night. Her skin warmed as images flashed through her mind. She tried to focus on something else as she turned off the bathroom light—she *had* to or else she wouldn't get any work done today.

Her laptop sat on a small desk in the corner of the room, ready for her to log on and become Miss Behavior. A white envelope sat on top of it.

Her name was scrawled across it in a bold, male handwriting she had to assume was Will's. A small, fuzzy feeling settled in her stomach at the thought of Will leaving her a note.

She slid her finger under the flap, but instead of a letter, she found a check. A check made payable to her for an obnoxious sum of money.

The fuzzy feeling died and she sat with an unladylike thud.

Rationally her brain knew the check was payment for Evie's training. She had a contract with Will for her services, and here was payment in full. They had a business arrangement, after all.

Emotionally, though, she felt she'd been kicked in the stomach. Leaving a check in her bedroom after the weekend—hell, after the *night* they'd just shared—made her feel cheap. Like Will was paying for a completely different type of service.

Ugh. *I guess I should be glad he didn't leave it on the nightstand.*

The rational part of her brain tried again. *He had to leave it somewhere. Why mail it to your P.O. Box when you're living right here? He's not paying you for sex. Remember, he said business and pleasure were two totally separate things. Get it together, go to the bank, and deposit it so you can pay bills this month.*

She still felt a little sick, even with the "let's be rational" pep talk. She slid the check into her purse and sighed. This was yet another reason she shouldn't have gotten involved with Will.

Gwen refilled her coffee cup in the kitchen, then turned her cell phone back on. She really should return Sarah's calls before Sarah sent the police over to check on her.

She flipped open the phone and her jaw dropped in shock. Twenty-two missed calls? Twelve new voice mail messages? Eight text messages? Good God, did someone die? She started scrolling through the missed calls log, noting most of them had come in within the last couple of hours, and nearly dropped the phone when it rang in her hand.

"Hey, Sar—"

"Why haven't you been answering the phone? Are you okay?" Sarah's rapid-fire pace didn't leave her time to answer any of the questions. "I tried to call yesterday, and then after I saw *Lifestyles*—"

"Slow down. What are you talking about? I turned—I mean, my battery died yesterday, so I'm just now checking my phone."

"So you haven't seen *Dallas Lifestyles* today?" Sarah's tone made her heart drop.

"No. Why?"

"Page three, Gwennie. You made page three."

Oh, *no.* Gwen sprinted to the kitchen and grabbed the glossy magazine. Page three was Tish Cotter-Hulmes's page.

Every Monday and Thursday Tish dished the hottest gossip and reported all the rumors on page three. No one wanted to make page three. Ever. Nothing good ever came of being on page three.

The headline stopped her heart. Is Miss Behavior Misbehaving With Dallas's Most Eligible?

"I'll call you back." She closed the phone on Sarah's sputtering and scanned the page. Oh, dear God.

Rumor has it that our own Miss Behavior may be vying for a new title. Sources tell me Gwen Sawyer moved in to Will Harrison's penthouse just last week, and there's no way she's only housesitting. In fact, Gwen and Will were spotted (along with Will's sister, the newly arrived and very elusive Evangeline) dining at Milano's on the West End and sharing popcorn at a movie afterward. Gwen and Evangeline were also spied having a very girly day of shopping and coiffing Friday, so I'm thinking there's definitely something going on. We all know how big a step shopping is. Personally, I'm intrigued. How did Gwen and Will cross paths and when? How have they managed to keep a low profile long enough for things to progress this far? Could Will be not-so-eligible any longer? Or is our Miss Behavior just flavor of the month? Anyone who can shed some light on the beginnings of this *affaire de coeur* needs to call me, quick!

In related news, the reports from Neiman Marcus say Evangeline spent a small fortune in a few hours with a personal shopper while Gwen supervised. Could this mean we're finally going to meet the Harrison heiress soon?

Several more paragraphs followed, each one more specu-lative than the last, all of them managing to put the worst possible spin on the slim details. Damn Tish! Gwen's fingers itched to wring Tish's scrawny, BOTOX-enhanced neck. Suddenly, the rash of missed phone calls made sense.

The anger receded as a chill settled over her. Not again.

Flavor of the Month? Her reputation could handle mild speculation about a possible romance, but to paint her as just another fling in a long line of flings? Especially one who had moved in? Once again, she was on the short end of the stick—Will's reputation was fine, while hers was tarnishing rapidly.

Romance or fling, one fact didn't change: the conservative elite of Dallas society wouldn't smile kindly on Gwen living with a man she wasn't married to. It didn't matter that it was the twenty-first century. As a debutante trainer, her moral compass needed to gravitate toward the 1950s—at least as far as her clients were concerned. It was unfair, yes, but a fact she'd come to accept as just part of the territory.

And Will would be livid. While his business—both personal and professional—ended up in the papers more often than not, she'd realized over the past week how much he tried to avoid the limelight whenever possible. In the past, Tish had limited herself to merely reporting Will's social life, but this time, she had moved to speculation and innuendo.

This was bad. At least Tish kept the speculation about Evie to a minimum. It was one tiny point in Tish's favor. Still, though, this was *bad*.

Tish better hope she didn't need any favors from Gwen anytime soon. Old Money was a small and closed society, but then so was the world of those who made careers on the fringes of that society.

Damn, damn, damn! Sarah had been right from the beginning. She should have thought this through more thoroughly before she signed on. Now she was hip-deep in trouble. She paced the kitchen, berating herself and feeling like the world's biggest idiot.

Calm down. It could be worse. Right now, it was just speculation and gossip. There was no proof she and Will were any
kind of item—fling or otherwise. No one, not even Sarah,
knew their business relationship had crossed a line. Well,
Evie might suspect something... It was only her own conscience reading damnation into Tish's column.

The one-two punch of Will's check and Tish's column made
her want to crawl back into bed and start the day over again.

But she couldn't. She'd had five years to think about
what she *should* have done when David hung her out to dry,
and slinking away in disgrace had been the worst possible
choice. She wouldn't make that mistake again. It was
damage control time. Gwen shuddered to think what waited
in her voice and e-mail boxes. And the messages on her
business line at home...

She took a deep breath and let it out slowly. Neiman
Marcus and the West End were both public places. *Anyone*
could have seen them and tattled to Tish. Plenty of people had
to have seen her coming and going from Will's building.
Everything could be explained away easily—provided she
could figure out how to explain without violating her nondisclosure agreement.

She'd have to call Will. Something she didn't look
forward to.

Will didn't want to expose Evie to the possible embarrassment the implication having a personal etiquette tutor could
bring. So how was she going to explain living here and taking
Evie shopping? She needed to have *some* rationale or everyone would accept the most obvious explanation for their
current living arrangement. And that was the absolute *last*
thing she needed.

She'd call Sarah back and see which way the wind was
blowing. Then, she'd check her messages and judge how bad
the damage was.

She wasn't going down without a fight this time.

* * *

"We'll need to arrange a dinner for after the meeting. Something regional would be nice." Nancy, fully recovered from whatever kept her out of the office on Friday, was back and trying to get him to commit on several projects—including final arrangements on his meeting with Kiesuke Hiramine. And though he knew he should be far more involved in this conversation, he found himself oddly uninterested. Too many other things on his mind. Like the memory of leaving Gwen in a tangled heap of sheets early that morning. Like the knowing look Evie wore at breakfast. Exactly *what* Evie thought she knew was a question mark, though.

"Sounds good. And?"

Nancy shot him an impatient look. "I also understand Mr. Hiramine is a golf fanatic. I'm making arrangements for him to play at your Club and at Brookhaven."

"Tell Matthews he'll need to be there for the golf outings. He's good at throwing a game." His phone rang and he glanced at it. He'd had his daily phone inquisition with Marcus, so that left either Evie or Gwen.

"I already have. And Mr. Matthews has the final sales and profit projections ready for your review."

"Excellent. Anything else?" Evie should be with her French tutor. That narrowed it down considerably.

"Your phone is ringing." Nancy was secure enough in her position to lob one parting shot as she gathered her notes and made a hasty exit. "I'll just leave these reports for you to look over later."

"Will, it's Gwen. Do you have a minute to talk?" The easy warmth that moved through him at the sound of her voice faded at the tension he heard in her words.

"Of course." It wasn't an entirely true statement, but the reports could wait a few minutes longer.

"Have you read today's issue of *Dallas Lifestyles?*"

"I never read that rag, but—"

"Tish Cotter-Hulme has half a column about us. I mean,

about you and me and Evie, and why we've been spotted together. I'm so sorry, Will. Tish is making all kinds of speculations…"

"Calm down. I'm fully aware of what she had to say this morning. I don't have to read it myself to get a full report of what she says about me. I have people for that." Gwen didn't laugh at his lame attempt at humor. "Just don't worry about it."

"*Don't worry?* Have you lost your mind?" Gwen's voice rose an octave, and he winced in pain. "You don't realize how many phone calls I've fielded this morning. Between people wanting me to confirm or deny Tish's rumors and my clients…"

"This is when the phrase 'No Comment' comes in handy." Why on earth was Gwen so worked up over a gossip column? "It's just gossip."

"Gossip kills careers like mine, Will. You may not read Tish, but other people do. And those people don't like the idea of a loose woman teaching their impressionable daughters." Gwen had herself worked up into a fine fit.

"A loose woman? Seriously?"

"I'm living in your *house*. The implication is that we are sleeping together."

"But we are…"

"That's beside the point." Gwen was practically sputtering.

"How is that—"

"I have to tell my clients something. *Some* reason why I'm living with you and Evie."

"Don't tell them anything. It's none of their business."

"Sadly, it is. Reputation is everything in this business, and mine is getting dragged through the mud. What am I supposed to…"

"Gwen, calm down. You can tell them you're working for me—I don't care about that. I just don't want people knowing the particulars. It would be embarrassing for Evie."

"*Hel*-lo, what else would I be doing other than tutoring Evie?"

"I don't know. You do business seminars, too, right? Tell

them it's related to HarCorp." Gwen made an odd choking sound. He assumed she objected to the small lie. "We sponsor the Med Ball, so it's not that far from the truth."

"And why I'm living with you?"

"That's easy. You're living with *us* so you can concentrate fully on your current project."

"But—"

"What's that line you told your readers to use when folks want to confirm gossip? Something about assumptions?"

"'What an interesting assumption'?"

"That's the one. If someone wants confirmation of Tish's implications and you don't want to go with 'No Comment' then use that line. Or that 'How kind of you to take an interest' one."

"You read my TeenSpace page?" Amazement tinged her voice. It beat panic, hands down.

"Well, Evie lectured me on my BlackBerry usage, so I thought I should check on the etiquette laws."

"I think I'm flattered."

"You should be." He smiled. At least she was starting to calm down. "Now, are you finished hyperventilating over this?"

"I guess." Gwen sighed. "You don't sound very upset over Tish's rumor mongering."

"I learned a long time ago to ignore speculations made about me and my private life. Tish just hasn't gotten the hint yet." Although with Evie on the scene, he should probably make clear that his willingness to ignore was very limited when it came to his sister.

"I thought you'd be livid. Or angry. Or at least irritated." Gwen's outraged sails seemed to have lost their wind, and her voice lost the last of its bluster.

"Oh, I'm irritated all right. It just doesn't do any good. That said, I try to avoid being fodder for Tish—or anyone else— as much as possible."

Gwen sighed again. "I guess I can make do with the minimum amount of excuses. Whether anyone will believe them is a different animal entirely."

"Good. Now can we talk about something else?" He leaned back and propped his feet on his desk.

"Don't you have work to do?"

His e-mail pinged. "Of course, but I have a few minutes for you."

"Now I *am* flattered."

"You should be. I'm a very busy man," he teased.

Gwen's chuckle sent heat rushing through him and all of his blood south. It was hard to believe just a week ago, he hadn't known this woman existed. Seven days later, he was ignoring HarCorp just to talk to her.

"Well, I happen to be a very busy woman. *You* may have time to chat, but *I* have clients to soothe and teenagers to counsel."

Will was oddly disappointed. "Good luck with that. I'll see you tonight."

"Bye."

With the phone in its cradle, he opened his e-mail. Another file on Japanese business practices and culture from Nancy. He sighed; he really needed to get Gwen to help him with his language lessons.

Gwen spoke Japanese. That sparked a memory from Gwen's first dinner. What had she said? Something about a degree in International Affairs? Yeah, and a special interest in Asian culture.

Why hadn't he made the connection before? *Because at first you were only focused on Evie, and then you focused too much on Gwen.*

He'd ask Gwen if she'd be willing to help him with this meeting with Hiramine. That would save him a ton of work. Less work also meant more time with Gwen. Plus, the time he spent working with her on this project…well, that line between business and pleasure he'd bragged about was getting thinner by the minute.

CHAPTER NINE

THE next few days passed in a blur for Gwen. Sometimes it seemed like a rainbow-colored blur, so perfect she felt she'd stepped into someone else's much-more-exciting and perfect life.

First had been Will coming home on Monday with a business proposition for her: consulting on the upcoming meeting with the Japanese company HarCorp wanted to join with in its Asian expansion. She'd wanted to squeal with the excitement.

Suddenly there weren't enough hours in the day to be Miss Behavior, Evie's etiquette tutor and Will's consultant and Japanese tutor. But both Harrisons managed to excel at whatever she threw at them.

Gwen never had a doubt Evie would shine socially, but the surprise came as Evie took an interest in the family business and quickly showed business savvy was an inherited trait. Family dinners moved from the basics of table manners and polite conversation to proper discourse on current events and HarCorp company business. Evie managed to retain her natural exuberance and charm while acquiring a polish fine enough for the most critical of society's elite. With her good looks and intelligence, Evie was destined to set Dallas on fire.

While Will picked up Japanese with a speed that impressed her, he chafed against the strictures of Japanese etiquette, his frustration at not being able to "cut to the chase" more than evident. But Will was a consummate businessman, and he didn't need any help in that department. Aside from a reminder to put the BlackBerry on silent, of course.

Both Evie and Will would be great successes on her résumé.

But for someone who'd always measured her happiness by professional success, Gwen couldn't deny that the best part of her day now came after Evie went to bed. Once Evie's door closed, Will transformed from charming boss and loving big brother into a bedroom-eyed Romeo intent on charming her in every way—including in her bed.

And she wasn't naive enough to believe Evie was ignorant of her and Will's relationship. No fifteen-year-old went to bed *that* early on a regular basis. Although she and Will tried hard not to make the physical side of their relationship blatant, Gwen knew Evie intentionally gave them privacy in the evenings.

Gwen didn't know where she and Will were headed—if they were headed anywhere at all—but she told herself she didn't care. Will never mentioned a future beyond the end of her contractual obligations, but they were all so focused on the events of the next few weeks, she couldn't read anything into it. She was living in the minute—enjoying what she could while she could. Gwen adored Evie, and her feelings for Will got more complicated every day, but she was taking her sister's advice to just take one day at a time. So far, that plan was working quite well.

Only one small problem flawed her otherwise halcyon existence—Tish's innuendos. She hadn't mentioned the column to Will or Evie since Monday night, but the fallout from Tish's gossip hadn't been pleasant. Two clients had backed out of their contracts already—one for a series of classes at a private elementary school and the other for a military wives' event. It took fancy footwork on her part to calm the sponsors of two of the debutante clubs that formed the backbone of her deb business. Half-truths and cajoling—and a little questioning of

Tish's sanity and sources—managed to pacify the most conservative of her clients, if only temporarily.

She'd taken the opportunity to instruct her TeenSpace readers on the inappropriateness of speculation and evils of spreading gossip. She was also ignoring Tish's e-mails outright.

By Friday, the furor caused by Tish's column had calmed for the most part. Life was good. And when Evie returned from her afternoon swim with an enormous smile and an even bigger favor to ask of Gwen, she just couldn't say no.

At seven forty-five—the first time Will had worked late in two weeks—Gwen finally heard the front door open and close and the rattle of Will's keys as he dropped them on the hall table.

"Anybody home?"

"In here," Gwen called from the den where she'd been nursing a glass of Merlot for the last half hour and watching TV.

Will rounded the corner looking slightly disheveled and completely adorable. Her heart skipped a beat at his smile. "It's awfully quiet. Do I want to know?"

She laughed. "No drama." *Yet.* "Mrs. Gray needed to leave early, so your dinner is warming in the oven. Evie is in her room."

"Really?" One eyebrow raised with the question. "Then I can do this." Without warning, Will leaned down and kissed her. A simple "Honey-I'm-home" kiss that seemed perfectly right at the moment and sent a happy little thrill through her. "How was your day?"

"Great. And yours?"

He grunted.

"That good, huh? Can I get you a drink?" He nodded, and Gwen went to the bar feeling oddly domestic at the *Ozzie and Harriet* scenario as Will loosened his tie and got comfortable on the couch.

Will rubbed his temples. "Is Evie sick?"

"No. I'm pretty sure she's on the phone." That was almost a given, considering. "Why?"

"Then I'm not sure I want to know why she's in her room this early. Do I even want to ask?"

Perceptive man. She took a deep breath. "Evie wanted me to talk to you about something."

"Uh-oh." He took the glass she proffered and nodded his thanks. "I'm not going to like this, am I?"

"Why would you think that?"

"Because she'd be in here otherwise, pestering me to death if it was something simple like a new phone or clothes. Instead she's put you up to it." He cut his eyes sideways at her as she sat. "She's smart, you know. You can talk me into almost anything. Plus, she figures if you're on her side, I'm bound to give in to whatever it is."

Gwen shrugged. Good Lord, she was picking up Evie's bad habits.

"You might as well hit me with it. I promise not to shoot the messenger."

Gwen mentally crossed her fingers. "Evie met a boy—a young man, I mean—at the pool today. He's asked her to the movies tomorrow night."

Will sat his glass down carefully and rubbed his eyes. "And?"

"And?" Gwen wanted to hit him with something. "There is no 'and.' Evie's been asked on a date and she wants to know if you'll let her go."

"Who is this kid?"

"Peter Asbury. Evie says he's sixteen and lives two floors down."

He nodded, but his expressionless face kept Gwen from figuring out how he felt about this new turn of events. "I know his father. He's the head of something at the university."

"Dean of Students." Gwen supplied automatically. "Well?"

Will swirled his drink in his glass. "She's too young to be dating."

"She's fifteen. It's not out of the ordinary or anything." Will's dry tone bothered her. Evie expected him to go through the roof at the thought of her dating, which was why she'd conned Gwen into being the one to broach the subject. Gwen hadn't expected fireworks, but Will could be discussing the weather for all the lack of emotion in his voice. The idea of hitting him sounded better by the moment.

"What did you say when she asked you?"

"I didn't say anything." That wasn't entirely true. She'd shared Evie's teenage glee like Sarah had shared hers years ago. "You're the one who has to okay it, not me."

"I'm asking for your opinion, though. Do you think she should go? This is new territory for me."

Get used to it. Evie's going to have the boys eating out of her hand and you'll be beating them off with a stick for the rest of your born days. "Do I think she's old enough? Probably. Do I think she's ready? It's hard to say. Do I think she's dying to go? Yes, definitely."

Will sighed, the sound of a man who had resigned himself to the grim reality of a teenage sister teetering on the edge of boy-crazy. "I guess it was bound to happen eventually."

Gwen hid her smile behind her wineglass.

"I want to meet him first, though," he grumbled.

"Why don't you invite him to dinner tomorrow night before the movie. You can grill him on his intentions and put the fear of God in him before they leave."

Will perked up at her last statement. "Oh, I like that idea. Fear is a good thing. Anything else I need to know about before I talk to Evie?"

"Nope." Gwen wanted to do a little happy dance for Evie. Finally Evie could make some friends her own age.

"Evie! Get in here!"

Shocked at the heat in his voice, Gwen stared at Will.

Will winked at her. "No sense letting her think this is going to be easy."

She rolled her eyes. "Then I'll leave you to it."

Evie stuck her head around the door frame. "Yes, Will?"

"The Asbury kid?"

Gwen slipped past Evie and whispered "Good luck" as Evie fumbled for words. She repressed the urge to giggle as Evie straightened her shoulders but still seemed to slink in to the room to get Will's permission for something she desperately wanted. In the privacy of her room, though, she succumbed to the urge to both giggle and do her happy dance.

Feeling like the champion of teenagers everywhere, she logged in to her Miss Behavior e-mail, ready to sort out all the angst-ridden adolescents of the world. It kept her busy for the next half hour until Evie knocked on her door.

"He said I could go!" Evie's ear-to-ear grin was infectious.

"I'm so glad, sweetie."

Evie wrapped her in a hug. "Thanks, Gwen. I'm going to go call Peter and figure out what I'm going to wear tomorrow. G'night."

"'Night."

Chuckling at Evie's obvious glee, Gwen started work on her next column—about first dates in honor of Evie—and didn't look up until she heard another knock on her door.

She half expected Evie to come in with an armload of clothes, but seeing Will there wasn't exactly a surprise, either.

He closed the door and leaned against it. "You didn't come back out." She'd never heard him so disgruntled.

"Sorry. I didn't know you needed company."

"Evie disappeared to her room to call that boy back and you've been in here all night. I've been bored. And I had to eat dinner by myself."

This time she did laugh at his grumbling, and he looked at her sharply. "You find that funny?"

"For someone who ate either alone or in the company of his BlackBerry until a few days ago, you've certainly set up camp on the other side now."

He shrugged. He and Evie had so many of the same mannerisms that it had to be genetic. "What can I say? I'm getting domesticated."

Her heart flipped at the word "domesticated." It sounded so hearth-and-home and Will didn't sound the least bit upset with the idea. When he smiled at her and crossed the room to pull her into his arms, that little warm spot in her heart she'd been keeping alive but carefully corralled blossomed into something she could no longer deny.

Her rational brain argued it could be the biggest mistake of her life, leading only to heartache and regret. But rationality couldn't hold back the knowledge that raced through her with such clarity it couldn't be anything else.

God help her. She was falling in love with Will Harrison.

Intimidating the Asbury boy proved immensely enjoyable. Will didn't doubt for a second Evie would be home by curfew. Evie was shooting daggers at him by the time she left, and his shins would be covered in bruises tomorrow from Gwen's well-aimed kicks every time she felt he crossed a line at dinner.

From the feel of it, he'd crossed several.

If that's what it took to convince Peter Asbury to keep his hands to himself, though, then his bruised shins would be well worth it.

He helped Gwen clear the remnants of their dinner from the table. As she loaded glasses into the dishwasher, she shook her head at him. "You should be ashamed of yourself, Will Harrison."

"What for?"

"You know exactly what for. I hope Evie comes up with a suitable revenge for your behavior tonight."

"Hey, all she has to do to avoid it is not date. I'd be good with that."

She wiped her hands on a towel and leaned a hip against the counter. "You are in for a long, painful journey through Evie's adolescence. And I'm starting to think you completely deserve it." She tossed him the towel and indicated he should wipe off the counter behind him. To his utter amazement, he did.

Good Lord, he *was* becoming domesticated. He'd never held a conversation with a woman he was romantically involved with in a kitchen before—much less helped tidy it while he did.

Gwen was a far cry from the usual husband-hunting trophy-wives-in-training he was used to. Instead of Prada and diamonds, she wore faded jeans and a pukka shell necklace Evie had given her. And instead of the normal topics of conversation he was accustomed to, she was teasing him and talking about the kid. It was a cozy domestic scene probably being played out in millions of households across the planet.

It was odd. It was strange. Something nagged at him that he should be horrified, but he wasn't. It was oddly comfortable, and somehow seemingly natural.

Gwen cocked her head at him and raised an eyebrow. "Was all that big-brother caveman posturing *really* necessary?"

"Don't tell me you're going to side with Evie."

Her chin went up a notch. "On behalf of younger sisters everywhere, I think I should."

"You can't. We have to present a united front."

Her eyes widened, and he knew he'd said the wrong thing. Her next quiet words confirmed it.

"I don't get a vote here. I may side with Evie at heart, but I won't undermine your authority."

Not quite a slap in the face, but close enough for someone who was feeling rather domesticated mere moments before. "I value your opinion, though."

"Thank you, but it's more important that you and Evie come to an understanding. Evie needs to learn to come to you with her problems, and *you* need to be ready to deal with them. I won't always be here to play middleman. Evie seems to be in denial of that fact, but surely you aren't."

Will was no novice when it came to women. He'd been

propositioned in every possible way by women far more cunning than Gwen. He looked at her closely, but saw no artifice. Gwen didn't seem to be angling for anything. In fact, for all her tone indicated, she could be discussing the terms of her contract. Which in a way, he admitted silently, she was.

Maybe that was why her words left a hollow feeling in his stomach.

He hadn't gotten where he was today by playing dumb or avoiding risk, but he also knew when it was time to call his own bluff. Closing the distance between them in two strides, he backed her against the refrigerator and captured her mouth with his. He still wasn't comfortable with all these new emotions Gwen kept stirring in him, but he was willing to see where they might lead.

Gwen's arms twined around his neck as she leaned in to him. He heard her soft sigh as his lips moved to her neck, and something more primal than physical stirred inside him. He nipped gently at her earlobe and felt her shudder in response.

"Maybe I'm in as much denial as Evie," he whispered.

He felt her stiffen at his words, and her eyes flew open to stare into his with an intensity he hadn't prepared himself for.

She let a hand trail down his shoulder to his chest, resting her palm where his heart pounded.

A smile twitched at the corners of her mouth. "Sounds like you both need therapy." The challenge was there in her eyes and in her voice.

Only Gwen would mock him at a time like this. "If it's two against one, I'm thinking you're the one who's in denial. Maybe you should be seeking therapy."

"I won't argue with that," she said, as she rose up on her tiptoes to mold her body against his and kiss him again. Her odd choice of words bothered Will for a second, but the touch of her tongue against his chased those thoughts away.

His hand snaked behind her to cradle her head, and the

backs of his knuckles brushed against the cold stainless steel of the fridge.

Conversation in the kitchen was one thing. Sex was a different story. Without breaking the kiss, he scooped Gwen into his arms and carried her down the hall.

They had several hours before he had to be standing watch over the front door so he could intimidate Evie's date some more. Having the free time so he could be alone with Gwen was almost worth letting Evie date in the first place.

CHAPTER TEN

"YOU made page three again, Gwennie." Sarah seemed to be struggling to not sound too pitying about it. "I'm so sorry. I'd like to break that witch's fingers for you to shut her up."

Gwen shifted the phone to her other hand and got comfortable on the couch. Sarah was worked up enough over Gwen's lack of regular contact, and the addition of another page three appearance hadn't helped. This could be a long conversation.

"Thanks, but I'd rather not have to bail you out of jail for your Assault charge." Gwen glanced over at the latest copy of *Lifestyles* containing Tish's newest column of salacious rumors about her. "It's just gossip."

Sarah practically sputtered, and Gwen had to fight back a laugh. "You're not upset?"

Gwen thought about her discussion with Will and Evie that morning over breakfast, and said, "I'm irritated, not upset. Let her speculate. I am curious where she's getting her information, though."

Much of Tish's column simply rehashed last Monday's speculations, with an update about the Ranger game the weekend before and more comments on their living situation, but this week she'd managed to ferret out information about Gwen's contract as well.

"Not from me, Gwennie. You know that, right?"

"Of course. It never even crossed my mind."

"Any fallout?"

"Actually Tish did me a huge favor by relaying the contract details. My clients now claim to understand why I moved in here in the first place, and no matter how she tries to twist the facts now to look more scandalous, it looks like a business decision. I should really call her and thank her as well for mentioning the 'exorbitant' amount of money Will's paying me. I can raise my rates." She tried for a lofty tone, but a giggle escaped and ruined it.

"Well, something good should come from the garbage Tish spouts. How's Evie handling it?"

"Pretty good. It was slightly embarrassing for Evie to realize most of Dallas now knew Will hired an etiquette tutor for her, but once she realized it wasn't that different from being sent through debutante training classes like any other girl, she got over it. Anyway, she's still floating from her date the other night. It will take a lot to burst that happy bubble."

"And you? How's your happy bubble today? Based on the message you left on my machine, you were totally floating last night."

A warm glow moved through Gwen and a tingle settled in her stomach. "I've never been happier."

"You're falling for him."

"Yeah, I'm pretty sure I am." Admitting it out loud was tough, but with that admission, the tingly glow in her stomach spread.

"And the feeling is mutual?"

"Will hasn't said anything directly, but I'm cautiously hopeful. We're in a strange situation now because we kinda skipped a few of those early casual-dating steps when I moved in here, but so far everything's just perfect."

"So this is going somewhere then?"

Gwen couldn't stop the smile, but her sister couldn't see it so she was still able to hedge a bit. "Hopefully."

"As in 'somewhere permanent'?"

In her secret heart of hearts, she might be thinking in that direction, but only a fool would share that kind of information too soon. Especially to Sarah. Her sister would have her in for a dress fitting before the echo of her words faded. "Let's not jump ahead of ourselves, okay? It's only been a couple of weeks. I promise you'll be the first to know if this…um…"

"Warrants further planning?"

"That'll do. Plus, there's Evie—"

"Evie adores you. I'm sure she's ecstatic to think you and Will might get…umm…'warrant future planning.'"

Like a djinn summoned by the speaking of her name, Evie bounded in through the front door. Gwen jumped at the sound. All those times she'd lectured debutantes about how to enter a room, she never thought she'd be thankful for the teenage inability to open a door noiselessly. Even Sarah heard it on her end of the phone line. "Speak of the devil."

"Indeed. I'll talk to you later."

"Bye. And Gwennie?"

"Yeah?"

"I'm so happy for you, honey."

"Thanks. Me, too."

One look at Evie's glowing face told Gwen Evie hadn't been lonely during her swim. "How's Peter today?" she asked casually.

Evie giggled, the unmistakable sound of a girl in a crush when the crushee returns the sentiment. Gwen knew the feeling well—especially since she felt a crush giggle trying to escape all the time recently.

Nothing like a new relationship to bring out a girl's inner fifteen-year-old.

"Go change. You can tell me all about it over tea."

He had piles of work to do, and therefore shouldn't be leaving the office early, but HarCorp had lost its monopoly on his time and attention. It was a beautiful, not-too-hot afternoon, and he could surprise Gwen and Evie by taking them out for an early dinner and a movie.

Will's new desire to delegate left Nancy gaping and his VPs scurrying, but that was one of the perks of being the boss. He'd hire Nancy her own secretary if that's what she needed or bring another VP on board to pick up the slack, but he finally understood what had pulled his father from the day-to-day grind of HarCorp. Thankfully Will himself figured it out twenty years earlier than Bradley had and wouldn't waste these years on a company when he had people at home who cared about him.

Silence greeted him as he opened the door to the apartment. No music blaring from Evie's stereo, no TV on in the living room, no sound of Gwen and Evie practicing small talk over tea or pretending to mingle.

Where were they? The pool? Shopping? Heading down the hall, he heard the faint sound of Evie's laughter. He veered right, into the living room, and noticed the balcony doors were open. Evie and Gwen were outside with their backs to the apartment, and they obviously hadn't heard him come in.

Gwen had her feet propped up on the balcony railing, those pink things women used when painting their toenails woven between her toes. What looked like the entire stock of a small beauty supply company littered the iron table next to her. Evie stood behind Gwen, a comb in her teeth like a pirate's cutlass, braiding Gwen's hair into cornrows while Gwen painted her fingernails.

He'd heard of girls doing stuff like this, but he'd never witnessed it live. As he watched, Gwen groped blindly beside her for a bottle of water while Evie kept a tight grip on the braid she held.

"Ouch! Easy there, Evie."

"Sorry." The comb clamped between her teeth distorted Evie's words. "But don't wiggle or I'll drop it."

Neither of them seemed to notice as he slipped out on to

the balcony. He leaned against the glass door, oddly fascinated by this feminine bonding ritual.

Evie wrapped a rubber band around the braid and went to section off a new row. "So I'm still going to have to join a debutante class?"

"Not for a couple of years. Don't you want an official debut?"

He hadn't thought about a debut for Evie. He didn't even know where to start. Good thing he happened to have a deb trainer around.

"Hold this." Evie tapped the comb against Gwen's shoulder. "It just seems ridiculous. I mean, I understand why I needed instruction *now*. Dallas is completely different from home. What would I learn in a deb class that you haven't already taught me?"

"Ahh, there's more to being a debutante than just walking properly. Plus, you'll get the fun of the ball and everything."

"What kinds of different things?"

He wondered the same thing himself.

Gwen held up crossed fingers. "I can't tell you. It's Top Secret Debutante Information only learned in official debutante classes."

"Really?" Evie was obviously intrigued, and Will smothered a chuckle. He could almost see her brain trying to come up with possibilities. Gwen shrugged, and Evie's mouth gaped open. "You liar. There aren't any debutante secrets."

"You'll have to go to class to find out, won't you?"

"Will you be teaching the classes?"

"It depends. You'd have to ask Will where the Harrison family normally presents. If it's at Will's Club, then probably not. Theresa Hardin teaches that class."

"Maybe Will could get them to hire you instead."

He'd been thinking the exact same thing and was surprised when Gwen waved the comment away.

"Thanks, Evie, but no. I'm not looking to pick up any more deb classes."

"Oh, I forgot about you wanting to ditch the debs."

"It's not that I want to ditch them. I just want to do some different things. I'm trained to work with companies and professionals, and that's what I'd really like to do more of."

"Like stuff you're doing for Will's meeting?"

"Could you please quit saying 'stuff'? There are a thousand words in the English language far more accurate than 'stuff.' But, yes, exactly like the 'stuff' I'm doing for Will's meeting. In fact, I'd been lobbying HarCorp with proposals for months before Will hired me to work with you."

She had? It was the first he'd heard of it.

"Really?"

"Yep. I actually went to that first meeting with Will thinking it would be my big break into the corporate sphere. I got you instead."

Will thought back to their first meeting. Well, that explained a lot about Gwen's reactions that day.

Evie laughed. "That must have been a surprise."

"Definitely. But I took the job anyway—"

"Obviously."

"Sarcastic interruptions are unnecessary," Gwen teased.

"Sorry."

"As I was saying, I took the job anyway, because I hoped it might lead to more work with HarCorp. And it did in the end. The success of Will's meeting will be a big boon for my résumé. Working for HarCorp will open a lot of doors for me."

A cold rock settled in his stomach. Surely he'd misheard her and she wasn't just looking for a stepping stone.

"And the deb classes will go?"

"It depends. But *your* success, my dear, will be seen as due to *my* excellent instruction and means I'll be in high demand for social training. The Harrison name attached to my business will lift me to the top shelf."

Will couldn't believe what he was hearing.

"I thought you were the best already."

"*One* of the best, maybe. But as you've found out, the wealthy are a tightly knit social class that's hard to break into. Now that word is spreading that I'm the one doing Evangeline Harrison's social training, more folks will want to hire me just because Will did. I should really send Tish a thank-you note for her help spreading the word."

Evie laughed and started to say something more, but Will had quit listening. The cold rock had turned to an icy weight in his chest, and his fists itched to hit something. He slipped silently through the glass doors back into the living room.

That conniving little bitch. She'd been working him since day one; he just hadn't been looking carefully enough for the agenda. Damn it, he should have seen it. Gold diggers after his money and social climbers after his name were nothing new to him. Hell, he'd learned to spot them from the smiles on their faces. But a woman who used him simply to increase her business contacts…That was a new one. One he hadn't thought to look for.

What an actress. Gwen's good-girl-with-good-manners persona had him fooled. She must have thought she'd hit the jackpot when he stupidly allowed his penis to think for him. He'd never pegged her as someone mercenary enough to sleep her way into a better job—or a better bargaining position for her business. And he, stupidly enough, had thought her the answer to all his problems—first Evie, and now the Japanese expansion.

Oh God. Poor Evie. She adored Gwen. Practically worshipped her. She'd be crushed when Gwen left them both for fatter wallets or better connections.

"Mr. Will! I didn't hear you come in." He cut his eyes quickly to his left where Mrs. Gray stood in the kitchen doorway, but he was more concerned with the reaction on the balcony. Mrs. Gray had spoken loud enough for Evie and Gwen to hear.

Both of them turned enough to see him standing at the door. Evie waggled the three fingers not holding pieces of Gwen's hair at him. Gwen's face lit up with a smile that would have meant something to him five minutes ago. Now he knew it was just another part of her act.

"Hey, Will. Gwen's letting me put cornrows in her hair. They look good, don't they?"

He wasn't sure what to say. "If you say so."

"You're home very early today." Gwen tried to swivel further in his direction.

"Gwen, don't move so much."

"Evie—"

The ice continued to move through his body. "Evie's right. Stay where you are. I have a lot of work to do, so I'll be in my office."

Evie merely nodded, but he saw the confused look that crossed Gwen's face. *Good. Let her wonder.*

He retrieved his briefcase even though there was no work in it and retreated to his office even though he had absolutely nothing to do in there.

Dinner was a quiet, uncomfortable affair. As far as bad dinners went, it was almost as bad as the first one she'd sat through with Evie and Will—minus the BlackBerry and Evie's rough table manners. At least that first night, Will had a reason to be quiet and uncommunicative.

Something was bothering Will and she didn't have a clue as to what. Everything had been fine—better than fine—when he left for work that morning. Evie came to her wondering what was wrong, and the best she'd been able to come up with was a possible "bad day at the office." Evie wasn't convinced. Will stayed locked in his office until Evie finally pulled him out for dinner. Since then, he'd said approximately ten words to Gwen and only when she asked a question to him directly. His answers were terse at best and monosyllabic at worst. Will did do better with Evie's attempts at conversation, but it had been so strained, Evie had lapsed into complete silence ten minutes ago.

Time to practice small talk. "I spoke with Mr. Heatherton today."

Evie pushed her peas around on her plate. Will merely grunted. Okay, this was going to be harder than she thought.

"He wanted a progress report on Evie. I told him he would be very pleased with all she's accomplished. Not only with me, but with her other tutors as well. Her French is really improving."

That earned her a weak smile from Evie. Will still said nothing. Evie, good student that she was, picked up the conversational ball.

"I like French. I'm still struggling with geometry, though."

Will cleared his throat. "I know you're working hard, Evie. I'm sure you'll figure it out."

Goody. Twelve whole words. It was a start.

"Mr. Heatherton would like to join us for dinner on Wednesday. I've already informed Mrs. Gray." With a wink at Evie, she added, "I didn't think we had much of a choice."

"Marcus is always welcome here," Will snapped.

Gwen choked. "Of course he is, Will. I wasn't implying otherwise."

Evie tried again. God love the girl, she really had learned well. "I'm happy Uncle Marcus will be here. I owe him an apology from last time. I hope he'll be impressed."

Gwen paused to give Will a chance to respond, but as the silence stretched, she gave up. "I'm sure he will be, Evie."

So that topic was exhausted. Great. Gwen searched for another. "I made you an appointment for Friday afternoon to get your hair done. Patrick wants to do an updo with sparkles to go with your dress for the Ball."

Finally something managed to spark Evie's enthusiasm. "I can't believe it's almost here. Do you think I'm ready, Gwen? I mean, we've done a lot, but the mingling thing…"

"Don't panic. Just remember to be yourself and you'll do fine. You're as ready as I can make you, honey. You're going to be the belle of the ball. I promise." She reached across the table to squeeze Evie's hand in support.

"You're right, Gwen." Will spoke sharply, startling them both. Evie dropped her fork in surprise. "Evie *is* ready for the Med Ball, and I can't think of anything else you need to teach her." Something ugly tinged Will's words, making Gwen's stomach tie itself in a knot. "You've certainly done your job and then some. Therefore, I don't think your 'services'—" he practically sneered the word at her "—are required further. I know you're anxious to get back to your regular life and business, so we won't keep you here any longer."

His words hit her like a slap across the face. She opened her mouth, but no words would come out.

"Will!" Evie gasped, her eyes round in shock.

"Wh-wh-what?" she finally managed to stutter.

"Oh, don't worry, Gwen. You've done an excellent job with Evie, and I'm sure she won't mind being a walking recommendation for your business. I'm afraid, though, you won't be using my sister or riding my company's reputation in order to serve yourself any longer. Go write Tish her thank-you note."

Oh God. Oh God. No! Adrenaline surged through her veins, but she felt paralyzed as the full meaning of Will's cold words settled.

"It's over, Gwen. All of it. Pack your things and leave." Will dropped his napkin on the table and stalked out of the room.

Her chest felt tight, and she forced herself to take deep breaths. Tears burned at the corners of her eyes, and she closed them, but the image of Will's angry face still loomed in her mind's eye.

"Gwen, no. You don't have to leave. *Please* don't leave."

She opened her eyes to see fat tears rolling down Evie's cheeks. "It's okay, honey. Don't cry." If only she could follow her own advice. She felt a tear or two of her own escaping.

Will had overheard her conversation with Evie. His remark about Tish and the thank-you note at least gave her that much information. She tried to remember exactly what she'd said. A weight settled in her chest, making breathing difficult again. Evie's protestations were regulated to background noise as she replayed the afternoon on the balcony. She tried to put the worst possible spin on her words and realized exactly where Will was coming from.

Mrs. Gray stuck her head out of the kitchen to investigate and looked around in confusion at the sudden change in the dining room. She looked first at Will's empty chair, then wrapped Evie in a matronly hug. "What's wrong? What's happened?"

I feel like I'm dying. She took a deep breath to steady herself and swiped at her cheeks. "Just finishing up my business here. Thank you for dinner, Mrs. Gray. I have to go pack now."

"No!" Evie shouted.

Gwen stood and shook her head gently at Evie, trying to forestall another outburst.

"I hate him!" Evie ran from the room and down the hall. "Do you hear me, Will Harrison?" she shouted. "I hate you! I hate you!"

The slam of her bedroom door echoed through the apartment like a gunshot.

"I'm sorry to see you leave, Miss Gwen. You've been so good for Miss Evie."

"Thank you. And thank you for all you've done for me."

"My pleasure, Miss Gwen."

She didn't have much to pack. A couple of drawers, a few things on hangers, her toiletries. Her laptop slid easily into its bag, and her teaching sets fit back into their cases without a problem. She blessed the monotony of the movements as her brain was churning too much to allow her to concentrate.

The pain in her chest, though, nearly crippled her. Regardless of what Will thought he knew about her ulterior motives for working for him, he'd completely dismissed their fledgling relationship like yesterday's gossip.

That was killing her. She'd either been played by a player

who was simply taking advantage of a situation, or Will didn't care half as much about her as she did about him. Either way, she'd played the fool. Again.

And she'd be paying for it dearly.

CHAPTER ELEVEN

Dear Miss Behavior,
I was with a group of people from one of my clubs at school and they were talking trash about another girl I know (she's not in that club, btw). That girl found out about some of the things they said, and now she's really upset with me. I've known this girl since elementary school, and we're friends. I didn't mean for her feelings to get hurt. How do I apologize for something like this and get her to forgive me?
Signed, Big Mouth.

Gwen sighed. *That's the million dollar question this week. Wish I could help you, honey, but you're on your own.*

She'd called Sarah Monday night to tell her Letitia could come home now and promptly burst into tears. The rapid change of events left Sarah sputtering in shock, and she'd arrived half an hour later with Letitia in a carrier and vanilla fudge brownie Häagen-Dazs in hand.

Sarah's support helped a little, but not enough to soothe the ache that had settled in her chest. Tuesday morning, Letitia's yowling for her breakfast forced Gwen out from under the duvet with the unwelcome reminder that life goes on.

Throwing herself into her work passed the time but provided little satisfaction. Several possible new clients contacted her, but Will's hateful words—*"you won't be using my sister or riding my company's reputation in order to serve yourself any longer"*—echoed in her head and stung her pride. These clients had indeed come her way citing her work with Will and Evie—as reported by Tish—as their source.

She was possibly the most popular etiquette consultant in the state at the moment, yet she was completely miserable. She was also well aware that if Tish got wind of many *more* details, her popularity would go in the toilet faster than she could blink.

By Wednesday afternoon, her depression started to give way to anger. Will jumped to a conclusion without even giving her a chance to explain. She'd been caught so off-guard by his anger, she hadn't been able to defend herself.

Granted, nothing she said to Evie on the balcony that day hadn't been true, but she'd been judged and convicted over her seemingly Machiavellian plans without any chance to explain. He'd taken everything out of context. She and Evie had been teasing each other all afternoon. He just came in too late to understand the joke.

Eavesdropping. Something she didn't realize she needed to explain the evils of to a grown man.

Anyway, how stupid did he think she was? If she had meant her words in the way Will interpreted them, why on earth would she admit that to his sister, of all people?

The anger finally fueled her and she shook off the self-condemnation—if not the self-pity. She wasn't the only guilty party here. Will's claim of keeping business and pleasure separate proved itself to be utter garbage. She was mad at him for feeding her that line, and mad at herself for swallowing it.

And she was disgusted with herself for falling in love with him and foolishly believing he might feel the same way about her.

Righteous anger and self-disgust for her foolishness kept her from calling Will and trying to explain. He certainly didn't know her at all, or else he wouldn't have believed the worst about her on so little evidence. And she obviously didn't mean very much to him if he were willing and able to just cut her out of his life without looking back.

So she was stuck in an impasse, unable to bring herself to call Will to explain and risk having him hang up on her, but unable to just move on because she loved him.

Therefore, she was just miserable.

Evie had taken to e-mailing her twice a day, keeping her up-to-date on her French lessons, her geometry struggles, her dress fittings and, most importantly, her budding romance with Peter Asbury. News of Will, however, came rarely, and was always prefaced with some kind of derogatory remark. Evie was still steamed at Will, and if she was treating him in person to the ire he received in her e-mails, life at the Harrison home was chilly indeed. She was doing her best to respond to Evie without dragging her into the middle of the mess with Will.

It wasn't an easy task, and it only compounded her misery.

Letitia stalked into her office carrying one of the ears formerly attached to her beautiful bunny slippers. She dropped it at Gwen's feet and meowed.

"A gift for me?"

Letitia batted the ear with a delicate paw, and meowed again, obviously proud of her kill.

At least it wasn't a real ear. "Thank you. I'm very proud of you for killing the big bad bunny." With a purr, the cat landed in her lap and snuggled down in a contented warm ball. Gwen scratched her behind the ears. "Good kitty. At least you still love and appreciate me."

Oh, God. I'm turning into one of those crazy cat ladies. I should just give in to the cliché and adopt ten feline friends for Letitia to keep me company in my lonely old age. She allowed herself to wallow in the misery and went for more ice cream. Who cares if it's only ten in the morning? She had nothing better to do than get fat.

With that, she burst into tears. Again.

* * *

Will looked over the documents Marcus had faxed to him, and the rock in his stomach gained more weight.

He wasn't Gwen's first attempt at sleeping her way to success. Fueled by the gossip swirling around—and Evie's complaints about Gwen's departure—Marcus had obviously done a bit of digging into Gwen's past. And he'd found something: David Seymore, Gwen's former boss and lover. On the phone, Marcus made it sound like Gwen had been the biggest scandal since Watergate, but in looking over the facts, it didn't seem to be more than a blip on the city's radar. If anything, Gwen had been the scapegoat for the gross misbehavior and poor planning of her boss. The size, scope or cause of the scandal didn't bother him, but the news Gwen had pulled this stunt before made him more than a little ill. Her first attempt had ended in disaster, but that hadn't stopped her from making the most of the situation when it rose again. She'd almost pulled it off this time—hell, for all intents and purposes, she *had* pulled it off. Even with the gossip, Gwen seemed to have landed on her feet *and* gained some nice business publicity for her trouble.

He heard the front door slam. Evie was back from her dinner with Peter's family. She passed by the living room without acknowledging him and down the hall to her bedroom.

He wasn't surprised. In addition to having the Harrison temper, it seemed Evie also carried a grudge with ease. She'd quit speaking to him unless absolutely necessary after Gwen's departure. Now, after three days of silence, Will actually missed Evie's usual nonstop chatter. Dinners were cold, silent affairs and Evie refused to be in the same room with him at any other time.

Tired of the impasse, he followed her to her room and caught the door before she could slam it in his face.

"How much longer is the silent treatment going to last?"

"Until you quit being a butthead." Evie flopped dramatically on her bed and turned her back to him.

Okay, that wasn't much better than the deep freeze. "Gwen was using both of us. Better to end it now."

Evie flipped over and sat up, eyes blazing. "Don't say that about her. It's not true."

"Trust me, it is. Do you think she's the first woman who's tried to ingratiate herself into my life? She won't be the last, either. *You* should be taking notes. The users and the gold diggers will be coming out of the woodwork after you soon enough. I'm just sorry I didn't see it sooner. Before you got too attached." *And before I got attached.*

"You're not only a butthead, you're a stupid butthead."

"That's enough, Evangeline."

"Don't 'Evangeline' me. You're not my father."

He could cheerfully strangle her. "But I am your brother *and* your guardian *and* you live under my roof."

"I should have gone to boarding school," Evie grumped.

"It's not too late, you know. I'll get the brochures from Marcus."

Evie gasped, then her mouth compressed to a mutinous line. "I hate you!"

"Excellent. It'll give you something to talk about with your therapist when you're older."

"I don't know why Gwen liked you so much. You're such a—"

"Butthead. Yes, I know." How had he managed to get pulled into this debacle of a discussion? Had he actually said the "under my roof" line? God. Teenagers obviously caused brain damage to adults. He took a deep breath and tried to regain control of the situation. "I'm trying to tell you that Gwen— as wonderful as you *think* she is—was playing us for her own gain. I wouldn't be surprised to hear she was the source for all of that gossip in *Lifestyles*."

"And I'm telling you she wasn't. Wasn't using us *or* providing Tish with information."

As much as he didn't like the idea, maybe telling Evie what

he'd just learned would help her see the truth. "Evie, this wasn't the first time she's done something like this."

Evie's eyes narrowed at him. "Do you mean what happened in D.C. with her boss?"

"You know about that?" What had Gwen been teaching his sister?

"Of course I do. It's not something she's proud of, but she says it's important to learn from your mistakes."

"Mistakes? This wasn't a 'mistake,' Evie. This is a prime example—"

An overdramatic sigh interrupted him. "You know, I heard her tell Sarah how getting involved with you would be a really bad idea. I guess she was right." With that, she turned her back to him.

Well, that was a waste of my breath. "Marcus will be here in half an hour. Change clothes and put a smile on your face before he gets here."

Evie merely huffed.

"And I promise you, if you call me a butthead or play that silent game at dinner, you'll really wish you had gone to boarding school. Here, allow me," he added, as he slammed her door.

He needed a drink.

Fighting with Evie, as frustrating as it was, at least beat brooding over Gwen. It was even slightly more productive. Gwen made a fool out of him and hurt Evie in the process. He wasn't sure which crime was worse.

If Tish and her column were to be believed, he'd broken his fair share of hearts. Karma must be trying to even the score. Making him feel like a fool was just a bonus. Fighting with Evie over it had to be part of his penance.

All he could do was hope Evie behaved herself at dinner. He did *not* want to hash this out in front of Marcus.

With a sigh of disgust over the shambles one small brunette had made of his life, he went to change for dinner.

CHAPTER TWELVE

IN ORDER to quit self-medicating with ice cream before she couldn't fit in her clothes anymore, Gwen switched to Retail Therapy. With Sarah's discount, she treated herself to a set of obnoxiously high thread count sheets—the kind she'd grown accustomed to in the last few weeks living at Will's. Tonight, she'd sleep in luxury.

In an effort to help, Sarah also provided a bag full of samples from the cosmetic counters, including decadent bath salts in her favorite fragrance.

She'd soak. Then she'd sleep. This horrible week would be over, and she'd have a fresh start for whatever she decided had to happen next.

Pushing the door open with her foot, she blocked Letitia's escape. From deep in her purse, she heard Evie's ring tone. Knowing tonight was Evie's big night, she'd been expecting a call all day. Evie, bless her heart, had to be a bit nervous. Heck, she was nervous for her, but she intentionally didn't call because she didn't want Evie to think Gwen had any doubts about her ability to shine.

"Hey, there! Are you ready for tonight?"

"Nooo, I'm not. I can't do this." Evie sounded on the brink of tears.

"Honey, what's wrong?"

"I'm going to screw this up. I know I am. I need you, Gwen. Please come with me."

Gwen dropped her bags to the floor and settled the phone more comfortably on her ear. "I can't, you know that. I'm not a contributor." *And there's no way Will wants me to show.*

"You can be my date."

"Evie…"

"Will has a meeting tonight and won't show up until late and Uncle Marcus has to go early and I can't walk in there by myself!" A sob broke through, and Evie drew a ragged breath.

"Yes, you can. You're ready for this. You're a natural and everyone is going to love you." *Okay, now I know how Sarah feels every time I go through a personal crisis.*

"Gwen, please." Evie was working herself up into a full-scale fit. "*Please* come with me. You told me about those companion women who used to go with ladies to balls to chaperone them. You can be that if you don't want to be my date. I need you there, though. Don't make me do this alone."

What to say? "Evie…"

"Please, Gwen."

She was both a sucker and a fool. Evie's pleas tugged at her heart. The poor kid had every reason to be nervous, and at the rate she was going, she'd be a complete wreck by the time she arrived at the ball.

I'm going to regret this. No doubt in her mind it was a bad idea. Of course, knowing something was a bad idea never stopped her before. Hell, bad ideas were what had put her in *this* situation.

"Okay. Just calm down. You'll get all puffy and blotchy if you keep crying."

"Then you'll come with me?" The relief in her voice made Gwen want to cry for her.

"I'll come with you—but just for a little while until you feel comfortable." *Hopefully, that will be before Will decides to show up.*

"Thank you, thank you, thank you."

"You can thank me by pulling yourself together and knocking them dead tonight." *Oh, hell, what am I going to wear?*

"I promise I'll make you proud."

"You already do, honey. Now, what time?"

"Uncle Marcus is sending a car for me at seven. I'll have the driver swing by and pick you up on our way, okay?"

"That'll work. I'll see you then."

"Bye, Gwen. And thank you. Really."

Seven o'clock? Yikes, it was after five already. She dumped food in Letitia's dish with one hand and dialed with the other.

Sarah answered on the first ring—she'd been on high alert all week with ice cream at the ready, but Gwen didn't give her the chance to go into Support Mode.

"I need a cocktail dress, but nothing too fancy. And possibly shoes, unless the dress will go with those black slingbacks I have. You know, the ones with the rhinestones? Oh, and I'll need jewelry, too." Leaving Letitia happily munching away, she sped down the hall to the bathroom.

Confusion crept into Sarah's voice. "Gwennie, what's up?"

"Oh, hell, just set me up with the full ensemble." She wiggled out of her jeans and left them where they landed. "Can you do my hair, too?"

"Of course, Gwennie. Whatever you need. Now, when do you want to come in? We could make a day of it, get our nails done…"

Gwen juggled the phone so she could peel off her shirt. She twisted the taps on her shower to full blast and the pounding water made it hard for her to hear. "You don't understand. I need this *now*. Tonight. Hell, twenty minutes ago would've been excellent."

"What? Why?"

"Just find me a dress and get over here with it. Please. I'm going to the Med Ball and I have less than two hours to get ready and I have *nothing to wear*."

"The Med Ball? Really? Oh, Gwennie," she gushed, "that's fantastic. So you and Will—"

"No. Me and Evie." Sarah started to say more. "Look, I'm getting in the shower now. I'll fill you in on all the details when you get here. Hurry."

"I'm on my way. I know just the dress…"

"Thank you. Bye, now." She flipped the phone closed and tossed it on the pile of clothes at her feet.

Somewhere between exfoliating and shaving, she realized this wasn't the relaxing bath she planned. And this evening…so much for a calming get-your-head-back-together night in.

She'd deliver Evie to Marcus, hang around long enough for Evie to acclimatize and realize she would do fine and then grab a cab home. An hour, max. Hopefully Will wouldn't decide to show up earlier than planned and make a scene. Her ego couldn't handle his derision twice in one week.

Neither could her heart.

"Gwen! You look amazing!" Gwen twirled a little for Evie and mentally thanked Sarah one more time. Her one-woman fashion army arrived forty-five minutes after her phone call, bearing a midnight-blue gown and ready to coif. Even the voice in the back of her head chanting "Bad Idea, Bad Idea," had been slightly beaten down by the results Sarah produced. If a girl had to risk looking like a fool, at least she could be gorgeous while she did.

"Now, let me see you." Evie turned full circle, and Gwen's breath caught. "Trust me, honey, you're the one who looks amazing. No one would ever believe you were a tomboy surfer girl just a couple of weeks ago."

Evie smoothed the ice-blue silk of her dress. "I know. Do you like my hair?" She patted the complicated curls and twists.

"It's beautiful. As are you. But I think I miss the cornrows."

"Me, too." Evie sighed dramatically at the loss.

"Well, I think you both look fantastic," Sarah gushed, snapping pictures like a proud mama on prom night.

A small wave of disappointment moved through Gwen at the thought. Had things worked out differently, she would have helped Evie get ready for tonight. Instead Evie had dressed for her big night out all alone. It just wasn't fair.

She forced a smile she didn't feel. "Let's go."

Limos didn't cruise her neighborhood often, and the one sitting in front of her house had her neighbors gawking. Evie slid in, saying, "I'm so glad we practiced sitting and standing and getting in and out of cars gracefully."

"See, I told you so."

Evie giggled, but not nervously. Instead Evie projected confidence and a youthful sophistication Gwen wished she could bottle for her debs. The stressed-out girl who had called her two hours ago was gone, replaced by a stunning young woman who seemed ready to conquer the world. Or at least Dallas.

As the limo coasted to a smooth stop in front of the hotel, Evie reached over to squeeze her hand. "You'll watch for my signal and step in if I need you, right?"

"I'll keep an eye on you, but you're not going to need me. You'll see."

Evie smiled, and her face lit up the inside of the dimly lit limo. "Thank you again for coming with me. The moral support helps."

"Knock 'em dead, sweetie."

A moment later, Evie stepped from the car with the aid of the chauffeur and into the waiting crowd.

Feeling very much like a Regency duenna chaperoning her charge, Gwen trailed slightly in Evie's wake. She scanned the crowd, noting she knew most of the faces: debs she once trained, the parents of her current and future debs, people she knew from their pictures in the paper. Evie held her head high and smiled as Marcus Heatherton broke away from a group of society pillars and met her halfway across the room.

"Evangeline! You look lovely, my dear."

Evie beamed as she turned a cheek to accept his air kiss.

"You look very dashing yourself, Uncle Marcus." Evie reached for Gwen and pulled her slightly forward. "And you remember Gwen, of course."

She bit her lip at Marcus's look of utter horror. No doubt Will had told him enough to make him believe the very worst about her. She plastered a smile across her face and brazened it out. "Mr. Heatherton, it's nice to see you again."

Marcus quickly schooled his features into benign friendliness. "How unexpected, Miss Sawyer. I didn't realize you would be escorting Evangeline."

Evie stepped in smoothly before Gwen could answer. "I had to beg her to come. I wouldn't be here tonight without Gwen's help, and I wanted her to see how well I did."

Oh, Evie was good. Not much Marcus could say in response to that without sounding like a first-class snob.

"I'm sure Miss Sawyer knows many people here and will enjoy catching up with them. If you'll excuse us, I'd like to introduce Evangeline to some of her father's friends."

Well, that could have been worse. Dismissed, she watched as Marcus led Evie away, and then flagged down a server for champagne. Moments later, she was surrounded by familiar faces as her former debs greeted her with hugs and flashes of enormous engagement rings.

Tish Cotter-Hulme found her quickly as well. The friendly crowd dispersed rapidly as no one wanted to unwittingly provide Tish with fuel for Monday's column. Tish's graying hair was swept back from her surgically enhanced face, which barely moved as she smiled. "Gwen, dear, I'm so glad to finally see you at one of these functions."

That fake smile didn't fool Gwen for a second, and her former good mood turned sour. Gwen tried to find a light tone to cover. "No comment, Tish. I've been on page three enough recently, thanks very much."

"Oh, Gwen, don't be so harsh. You make it sound like I'm only after a story."

Gwen kept a surreptitious eye on Evie, who seemed to be doing better than fine at the moment. Bradley Harrison's friends and business cronies wore enchanted smiles, and since several had teenage grandsons Evie's age, Gwen wouldn't be surprised if Evie's social calendar filled up rapidly after tonight.

"If you weren't, you wouldn't be standing here." Gwen sighed. "For the record, there's no story to report. I was hired to help Evie transition from her old life into her new one. You know that. As you can see, she has done so beautifully. I'm only here because Evie asked me to come because she thought I might enjoy myself. I've grown very fond of her over the last few weeks, and I'm very pleased with how well she's handled all of the adjustments. Coping with the loss of her parents and a move here is a lot for anyone to handle and she's done beautifully." *There, print that on page three, you nosey witch.*

Tish cocked an eyebrow at her. "And Will Harrison? Are you fond of him as well?

Gwen lifted an eyebrow of her own. "I think you've beaten that dead horse long enough. Oh, I know how boring truth is compared to speculation, but you're just writing fiction these days." Evie was now being introduced to the president of the Dallas Junior League and the head of Parkline Academy. When she tossed her head back and laughed, Gwen knew tonight was a complete success. In another few minutes, she'd be able to head home without worry.

"But you—"

Inspiration struck. "I tell you what. You tell me how you found out about my contract, and—" she leaned in conspiratorially and lowered her voice "—I'll give you something for Monday's column."

Tish eyed her suspiciously. "What's in it for you?"

"I'm just curious."

"You're willing to violate your nondisclosure agreement just to appease your curiosity?"

How'd she know about that? "Let's just say there are some

things I know about the Harrisons that won't put me in violation of anything."

"Don't jerk me around, Gwen. It won't be pretty. Rumors kill in your business, you know."

"Oh, trust me, I know. I've done plenty of damage control thanks to you."

"Fine. Will Harrison had a temp in his office one day while his normal tight-lipped secretary was out sick. The temp found your contract and your check. She called me."

Good to know. She'd make sure Nancy had that tidbit of info first thing Monday morning. HarCorp's HR was about to be hit by a hurricane.

"So what have you got for me?" Tish practically salivated at the idea of juicy gossip she could twist into something even more salacious.

Gwen thought quickly. "From what I heard—" she smothered a smile as Tish leaned in eagerly "—Will isn't dating Grace Myerly any longer."

Tish's face fell. "That's it? Everyone knows they called it quits months ago. Old news, Gwen."

"Really?" She feigned innocence. "*I* didn't know that. It was a surprise to me."

"Surely you have something better for me."

Gwen shrugged. "Sorry, no. I guess I wasn't in as tight with the Harrisons as you insinuated."

"Don't play stupid, Gwen. It doesn't suit you." Suddenly Tish's attention shifted to something over Gwen's right shoulder. Her face lit up in interest. "Oh, look, there's your boss now."

Gwen froze. *Oh, no.* Why hadn't she left earlier instead of standing here sparring with Tish? She turned to see Will make a beeline to the crowd surrounding Evie. Will bent to kiss Evie's cheek in greeting, but Evie's response lacked her normal exuberance. Thankfully only someone who knew them both well would notice.

There was much handshaking and backslapping going on

around them, and Evie now wore a small, self-conscious smile. If she had to guess, Will was being made aware of how charming and what a success she was. Then, someone else said something, causing Evie to give Will a "so there" look, and Will stiffened slightly.

He knows I'm here.

When Will started to scan the crowd, Gwen knew he was looking for her. She really didn't want their first meeting to be here, in this crush of people. She hadn't yet figured out what she wanted to say to him.

"Who's he looking for, I wonder?" Tish's voice made Gwen jump. She'd forgotten Tish was still standing there, and the insinuation in the statement made Gwen want to smack her.

"Hmm, I don't know, Tish." She had to get away from that woman, so she added brightly, "If you'll excuse me, I think I'll get a refill on my drink."

Without waiting for Tish's response, Gwen headed for the bar. She cut around the dance floor, where couples moved easily to the band's music, smiling and waving to people like nothing was out of the ordinary.

She took a deep breath, and concentrated on slowing her rapid heartbeat. She hadn't prepared for this. Seeing him. Her chest hurt, and she vacillated between wanting to hit him with something heavy and wanting to run to the bathroom and hide. Leaving—while the obviously simple solution—wasn't an option now. Even if no one believed Tish's rumors of romantic doings between them, everyone knew of their business relationship. Etiquette required her to at least speak to him.

Sometimes, the rules really sucked.

The bartender handed her a fresh glass of champagne and she sipped at it gratefully. Each bubble, though, seemed to have taken on a sharp edge and made swallowing difficult.

"Gwen? You look pale. Is everything all right?"

It took her a second to focus on the speaker. When her brain clicked back on, she saw Megan Morris, the former debutante who gave her the nickname of Miss Behavior, staring at her with a worried expression.

"I'm fine now, Megan," she lied. "I just got a little over-heated in the other room."

Megan patted her arm. "It is a bit of a crush sometimes. Plus, I saw Tish Cotter-Hulme had you cornered there for a while. That's enough hot air to overheat anyone." She smiled, and Gwen's heart rate finally began to slow to a normal rhythm. "Now, come with me. I have some people I'd like you to meet."

She couldn't say no, so she allowed herself to be led to a group of twentysomethings where she made idle conversation for the next fifteen minutes. She tried to keep an eye on Evie, just in case, but Evie had made her mark and was taking a turn on the dance floor. She'd just managed to relax some when she saw Will approaching out of the corner of her eye.

She tensed as members of the group greeted Will. Finally Will turned in her direction, and she braced herself.

He won't make a scene in public, she reminded herself.

"Gwen, I didn't expect to see you here." There was no warmth in his voice, and her heart ached at the bland, yet polite, tone.

"It was a last-minute plan. Evie asked me to come." She watched the people around them carefully, but no one seemed to see anything amiss. "I assume Evie's having a good time, as I haven't had a chance to talk to her since we arrived."

"Evie seems to be enjoying herself, and she's certainly charming my father's friends. May I speak with you for a moment?"

"Of course." *Act normally.* "Excuse me," she said to the others, hoping they'd see nothing out of the ordinary about Will's behavior.

"Care to explain what you're doing here?" So much for bland-yet-polite—Will's tone could refreeze the ice sculptures.

"Marcus had to come early and you were going to be late and Evie didn't want to walk in alone. She shouldn't have been placed in such an uncomfortable position, and I couldn't deny her such a simple and understandable request." She raised an eyebrow, practically daring him to rebut.

The arrival of the chief of staff from the hospital forestalled Will's response, and she listened and smiled politely as Will and HarCorp were thanked profusely for their support of the hospital's fund-raising efforts.

When the chief of staff moved on, Will grabbed her by the elbow. "Let's dance."

Gwen felt her jaw drop. "What?"

"Don't get uptight. I'd like to carry on this conversation without interruption, and the only place I can see to do that is on the damn dance floor."

She sputtered, but managed to put one foot in front of the other until Will found an empty space on the dance floor and pulled her into his arms.

Her stomach clenched and her whole body ached from the sensation of being close to him. His tux made him look even more breathtakingly handsome than usual, emphasizing the breadth of his shoulders and the lean-muscled length of his body. Gwen inhaled the scent of his aftershave with each breath, and the hand she placed on his shoulder itched to caress the warm skin only inches away. It was torture and her heart was taking the brunt of it.

If Will noticed, he didn't say anything, and he certainly didn't seem to have a similar response to her. He kept the proper distance between them and continued their earlier conversation.

"So this was Evie's idea."

"Of course. Why else would I be here?" Gwen glanced around. So far, no one seemed overly interested in their appearance on the dance floor, but again, based on their prior business dealings, it shouldn't draw undue attention.

She hoped.

Will moved easily to the music. "Evie I can understand. She's been your most vocal defender."

Gwen stiffened. "I haven't done anything that needs defending."

He continued as if she hadn't said a word. "Bringing you here is Evie's thinly veiled attempt at forcing a reconciliation."

"Do you think I—"

"I'd hate to even try to guess how your mind works, Gwen." He sneered.

"That's uncalled for." *Enough.* Her feet froze. She wasn't going to fight with him on the dance floor in front of hundreds of people.

Will's hand tightened on her waist. "Keep dancing. You wouldn't want to make a scene, would you?"

She was fuming, but he was right in knowing she wouldn't intentionally make a scene. She forced her feet to move. The song couldn't last more than a couple of minutes longer, and then she'd be able to leave without drawing undue attention.

"So, do you deny that you only took the job in order to drum up additional business?"

At least that was an easy enough question. "It's called good business sense, Will. Every business owner hopes the current contract will lead to future ones. Surely you understand *that.*"

He shrugged. "Usually those contracts will be in the same general field. You decided to use my sister to infiltrate HarCorp. I checked with HR, Gwen. They had a file of your proposals."

"I'm not denying I lobbied HarCorp in the past."

"I just offered you the chance to do it in person."

"Which I never did! I agreed to work with Evie and that's exactly what I did. *You* came to *me* with the consulting job."

"Which was just what you wanted."

"Of course I did. It was the kind of opportunity I'd been waiting for for years." Will's jaw tightened. "Let me repeat— I lobbied HarCorp. I never once lobbied *you.*"

"You didn't have to. You just crawled into my bed for the job."

She gasped and her fingers itched to slap him for that gross insult.

"You are a first-class bastard." She caught herself hissing and plastered a smile back across her face for the benefit of their audience. "You're not the only one who can separate business and pleasure, you know. And, just to refresh your memory, *you* crawled into *my* bed."

"You never answered my initial question, Gwen."

"Which was…?"

"Did you take the job with Evie so you could weasel your way into HarCorp?"

"Absolutely no—" She stopped, thinking back to that day in Will's office. She had almost talked herself into taking the job simply for the possible "in" into HarCorp *before* she got the full story on Evie and made up her mind. But it had been such a brief moment, and she'd gotten attached to Evie so quickly…

Will must have noticed her hesitation and decided it was a guilty conscience. She saw his eyes harden as he confirmed his suspicions based on her momentary lapse. She was doomed no matter what she said.

"And where did sleeping with me fall in your business plan?"

"If you remember correctly, I told you that would be a bad idea."

"Seemed to work out pretty well for you. Of course, you've had plenty of practice, haven't you?"

She sucked in her breath. Was he referring to David? The sarcastic tone answered her question. *How* did he know about that? *Oh God, could this be any more horrible?*

"You almost pulled it off. If you hadn't gotten cocky, you might have milked me for more."

She stopped dancing, well aware of the stares they attracted, but not caring any longer. All of her training and all of her studies failed her. None of the speeches or explanations she practiced over the week worked in the face of being called something only slightly better than an opportunistic whore.

She'd been so used to Will looking at her with kindness and an endearing smile, the hardness that stared back at her all evening was breaking her heart. But when his face cracked into a mocking smirk, she wanted to scream.

"You're good, but you're not that good." With that, Will turned on his heel and left her standing alone on the dance floor, her mouth gaping in shock.

Evie appeared in her line of vision, her eyes wide and her face pale. Horrified, Gwen looked around her. While some people tried to act nonchalant, like nothing had just happened, she could tell by the body language that every one of them had seen Will leave her standing there. And it didn't take a crystal ball to see what would happen next. A woman in a red cocktail dress leaned to the woman on her right and whispered. Anyone who hadn't witnessed Will's act of rudeness would have a full reporting in no time.

Hot-faced and humiliated, Gwen tried to hold her head up as she left the dance floor. She even tried a smile and a shrug as if to say, "oh, well." It didn't work. She could tell by the stares of shock and pity.

The band, as if aware of the drama and sensing the need to change the subject quickly, launched into an upbeat swing piece. Gwen skirted the couples making their way on to the dance floor and looked for the nearest exit.

Tish waylaid her departure. "Seems you do hold up your end of a bargain. You promised me something good for Monday's column, and you certainly delivered," she said with a smirk.

That was the proverbial last straw. Every pithy and etiquette-approved remark escaped her. Nothing Tish could print at this point could be any more personally humiliating or professionally damning than the scene she'd just provided for everyone's entertainment.

"Bite me, Tish."

She didn't take any time to appreciate Tish's openmouthed shock, choosing instead to make her exit on that small high note.

The doorman flagged a taxi, and Gwen barked her address at the driver. In no mood for small talk, she stared out the window and tried to calm her whirling thoughts.

She never should have let Evie drag her to the Med Ball. In light of Will's statement about Evie's matchmaking, Gwen wondered if Evie's earlier panic attack had been nothing more than part of a larger scheme.

I never learn, do I? Tonight's debacle just drove home how stupid she was. At least she wouldn't have to wait long for the fallout. Tish would help spread the word to anyone who wasn't at the Med Ball—and from the look on Tish's face, Gwen was going to pay dearly for her comment in Monday's column. By Monday afternoon her humiliation would be complete. And if her clients had been willing to drop her at the first whiff of a scandal two weeks ago, the fact she was on the outs with the Harrison family would have her black-balled by Tuesday afternoon at the latest.

Tears burned behind her eyelids. She hoped she still had ice cream in the freezer.

CHAPTER THIRTEEN

EVIE'S silent treatment was total and absolute, and Will almost felt like he was living alone again. While she'd kept her game face on at the Med Ball, only shooting him a few dirty looks after Gwen left, she'd shut down completely in the limo on the way home. Comments, questions, attempts at normal conversation—everything was met with stony silence. Even eye contact was out. He'd never been so completely ignored in his entire life. She stomped to her room without looking back, and had only left it to eat for the rest of the weekend. Mrs. Gray had weekends off, so Will rattled around his apartment alone in the silence.

And it was driving him insane.

He worked in his office with the door open, just in case Evie decided to call a truce. While it gave him a chance to catch up on the paperwork he'd let slide the past couple of weeks, he derived little satisfaction from the work. It didn't help that the majority of his time was spent working on his upcoming meeting, and that meeting made him think of Gwen.

The sight of her at the Med Ball had nearly knocked him off his feet. He'd grown accustomed to a down-to-earth look for Gwen—battered, curve-hugging jeans or sundresses that flowed around her luscious legs. He'd even gotten used to those frumpy Miss Behavior suits she insisted on wearing. But Gwen as socialite, with her hair swept up to expose the long, lovely line of her neck and wearing a beaded blue cocktail dress that exposed just enough cleavage to remain classy yet still leave him salivating…that had set him back a pace, at least until the blood had started circulating freely again.

He tried to block the image of Gwen from his mind and concentrate on the work they'd done for the meeting. He had to give her some credit, however begrudgingly; she was more than a pretty face and amazing body. She was certainly good at her job. Gwen's notes on everything from the order of introductions to sketches showing where everyone should sit at the conference table were astoundingly thorough. Small notes written in the margins of his proposal outline in her precise handwriting showed she understood both the human and business aspects of successful meetings.

When he got to the page where she gave suggestions about what color ties he and his VPs should wear, he had to laugh. No detail was too small for her attention, it seemed.

He wondered if Gwen provided this level of service to everyone. If so, then her consultant's fee was too small. Thinking back to previous meetings and events, Gwen's expertise could have come in handy at HarCorp. Odd that HR never followed up on any of her proposals…

I lobbied HarCorp. I never lobbied you.

Gwen's words echoed in his head. That much had been true.

If he wanted to be honest with himself, he probably deserved Evie's silent treatment. He treated Gwen with unbelievable rudeness Friday night. He remembered one of her lectures to Evie: *"You don't have to be friendly. You don't have to be kind. But you do have to be polite. There's no excuse for flat-out rudeness. I don't care how angry you are."*

He'd let his anger take the lead and look where it had led him. She'd hurt him and he'd wanted to return the feeling. She'd used him to further her own ambitions—or at least he'd thought so. In the late nights after she left, he'd had a chance to rethink the events of the previous days and weeks and wondered if he'd jumped to an inaccurate conclusion. But seeing her at the Med Ball caused his anger to flare up again. All he saw was another woman riding his name—or in this case, Evie's feelings—for her own benefit. So he'd accosted her and blasted her with his worst suspicions.

The look on Gwen's face when he left her on the dance floor would stay with him for a long time. Whatever else she'd done, whatever her reasons were for working for him, she hadn't slept with him for professional gain. No one could fake the look of shock and hurt he'd seen in her eyes.

But if she was innocent of scheming and manipulations, then why hadn't she defended herself? She'd never had a problem taking him to task before. But she'd left without so much as a word and hadn't attempted contact since. Her silence should indicate she was guilty on all counts.

But now that he'd calmed down, he realized he couldn't have misjudged Gwen's character that completely. He wasn't a man easily fooled by anyone. His instincts had never been *that* wrong. He'd gotten his feelings hurt and jumped the gun in defense.

Which meant he may have screwed up big this time and run off the first woman who'd ever gotten under his skin.

In other words, he really was the butthead Evie accused him of being.

"I hope you're happy now, Will." Evie's first words since Friday evening blasted him as he came into the kitchen for his last cup of coffee before he left for work. She sat at the bar counter with a bowl of cereal in front of her and the newest edition of *Dallas Lifestyles* in her hand.

She couldn't have been more wrong. *Happy* wasn't in his emotional repertoire at the moment. But something had finally broken Evie's vow of silence—even if she was still angry.

He refilled his mug. "Good morning to you as well. I'm glad to see you're speaking to me again."

Evie snorted. "Hardly. I'm going to my tennis lesson." She

tossed the open issue of *Lifestyles* on the counter in front of him. "There. You should be pleased with yourself."

Evie huffed out of the room and he heard the front door slam behind her as she left for her lesson.

He sipped at his coffee as he read the Society Column for the first time. As expected, the article covered the who-wore-what and the other basics of the Med Ball, but moved on very quickly to a far more interesting topic.

I hate to say "I told you so," but that doesn't make it less true when it comes to the Miss Behavior/Will Harrison situation I've been following the last couple of weeks. Despite protestations to the contrary from all sides, I've been firm in my assertions that Gwen Sawyer and Will Harrison had something going on when she moved in to his penthouse. Things have certainly turned interesting, and current events shed new light on the older facts. First, news trickled in that Gwen moved out very suddenly early last week, and the "friendly" relationship between all parties cooled considerably. Certainly, the lack of sightings about town seemed to confirm that. Miss Behavior's arrival at the Med Ball in the company of Evangeline Harrison might have thrown everything into question, but the Sawyer/Harrison showdown witnessed by yours truly and the other three hundred guests was nothing short of a lover's spat. No one has come forward with an account of what was said, but one thing was perfectly clear when Will left Gwen standing alone on the dance floor: her services—whatever she was providing—are no longer necessary or welcome. It leaves one to wonder if Miss Behavior has lost her magic touch.

He read on in disgust. Tish Cotter-Hulme was out for blood—mostly Gwen's for some reason. While speculation about his side of the story was kept to a minimum, Gwen got dragged in the mud both personally and professionally.

No wonder Evie had broken her vow of silence just to condemn him. If Gwen caught fallout from the earlier speculations and rumors, she was living on Ground Zero right now.

The last paragraph caught his eye.

Society-at-large finally got to meet the elusive Evangeline Harrison at the Med Ball, and she represented the Harrison family with style and class. Evie, as she is known to family and friends, is a breath of fresh air and a charming young lady. In an ice-blue silk…

Not that he'd had any question about Evie's success, but here it was in black and white for everyone to see. She should have been basking in the good press and enjoying her moment in the society column sun. Yet Evie hadn't said a word about it. After the crucifixion of Gwen in the paragraphs before, he could see why.

The morning traffic gave him even more time to think. The more he did, the nagging suspicion he'd not only judged Gwen harshly and unjustly but then compounded the issue by humiliating her in public intensified.

He could cheerfully wring that gossip woman's neck for her speculations. However true they were, it still wasn't for her to make them public. Plus, the viciousness in her attacks against Gwen went beyond the simple desire to sell papers. Tish's attacks were personal; Gwen had made an enemy of the woman somehow.

Legally there wasn't much he could do about it since gossip wasn't a crime—no matter how malicious he thought it was—and he couldn't go calling the paper without making the situation worse. But surely HarCorp's legal team and advertising department could stir up enough trouble at the paper to make that woman think twice before dragging Gwen through the mud again. It would probably keep her away from Evie as well.

The thought of turning his people loose on Tish Cotter-Hulme and her ilk gave him a great sense of satisfaction. That satisfaction sparked another realization in him he wasn't quite ready to deal with yet.

Gwen was more than just under his skin.

"Just quit answering the phone, Gwennie."

If I did, would you quit calling, too? Gwen didn't voice the frustration because she knew deep in her heart that Sarah only meant to help and console with her every-ten-minute phone calls. Didn't Sarah have actual work to do today?

But the headache pounding behind her eyes wasn't Sarah's fault, so Gwen tapped into her last reservoir of patience for her sister. "I can't. Silence is perceived as a sign of guilt. If I'm going to salvage what's left of my reputation and business, I have to have good explanations for Tish's accusations." Another message pinged into her in-box and Gwen sighed. "At least I can copy and paste the same thing over again in the e-mails."

To call the morning "hellish" would be an understatement. If she could keep reminding everyone how much Tish liked to blow the smallest of issues out of proportion and thereby make her "showdown" with Will seem like it was taken out of context simply for the dramatic effect, she just might make it through this with her career intact, if slightly battered. Thankfully many of her clients had been dragged through Tish's mud pit at some point, and they were proving somewhat sympathetic to her plight. Some carefully worded comments and a light tone helped.

So the hellish nature of her morning stemmed more from her own heartache than Tish's column. Yes, the damage control was taking its toll on her nerves and patience, but it was the constant discussion of Will that had her stomach in knots.

"How are you holding up, Gwennie?"

"Better than you, it seems."

"I can't help but worry."

Sarah sounded close to tears, and Gwen instantly regretted her snappish tone. "I know. And I appreciate it. But nothing has changed since last week other than the public nature and level of my humiliation."

"*Call him.* Call Will and explain."

Gwen sighed. "At first, I wanted to, you know, but I couldn't pull myself together to do it. But now I'm angry. *He* jumps to conclusions and berates me. *He* acts like a jerk and embarrasses me in public, yet I'm the one catching the flack. Even if he deserved an explanation, I'm not inclined to provide one anymore. I'm not sure I ever want to speak to him again."

"I don't believe that for a second."

"Start trying." When yet another e-mail pinged into her box, she saw the president of the Junior League's name in the sender line and cringed. She closed her e-mail program and headed for the kitchen for coffee.

"So you're willing to walk away from what could be the one guy you've been waiting for your whole life because of this?"

Gwen didn't have a ready answer. Letitia twined around her ankles and purred loudly as she refilled her cup for the umpteenth time this morning.

"At least when David hung me out to dry he had reason to—even if it was a purely selfish one. Plus, I brought a lot of it on myself with my naiveté. But this... There's just no excuse. Will doesn't trust me. He believed the worst about me and condemned me on the flimsiest of evidence, then compounded it by humiliating me in public." She'd followed her heart and her hormones and been so swept up by Will, the realization that crashed down on her was killing her. Her heart cracked and her voice broke.

"He's not the guy I've been waiting for."

CHAPTER FOURTEEN

"MR. HARRISON, I'm afraid there's a small problem."

Will looked up from the quarterly reports and saw Nancy hovering in the doorway between his office and hers with a worried look on her face.

"Just tell me it has nothing to do with Kiesuke Hiramine, the meeting, or anything Japanese in nature," he joked. Hiramine's flight was already in the air, and he and his team would be arriving tomorrow. Everything was in place for Friday's meeting, all the way down to the high-gloss shine on the conference room table.

"I'm afraid it does."

Damn. "What happened?"

"You asked me two weeks ago to find you an expert on Asian business and culture to assist with the meeting. When you hired Miss Sawyer as a consultant, I assumed she would be present and no one else would be necessary." Nancy took a deep breath. "I realized Monday that would no longer be the case, but I'm having a very hard time finding a replacement on such short notice. I've found a translator who's available Friday, but he has no other qualifications."

Nancy wouldn't be standing in his doorway if she thought a translator would be good enough, and she wouldn't be giving him the entire spiel unless she had a solution in mind.

He waved her into the room and leaned back in his chair. "So what do you suggest?"

"Bringing Miss Sawyer back on board is the simple and obvious solution. She is already familiar with the situation and she certainly has the expertise necessary. Unless, of course, your, um, personal relationship with her makes that a completely unacceptable choice."

"I see." Gwen *was* the obvious choice. The question was would she do it?

"I need to call the caterer back, so I'll leave you to decide. Let me know if you'd like me to call Miss Sawyer or book Mr. Michko simply as a translator."

Will tapped his pen on the desk. Hiring Gwen back would certainly solve his immediate business problem. And there were other benefits, too. It might not completely thaw Evie's cold shoulder, but she might lighten up. It would also help Gwen counterbalance the gossip about her and her business. Going back to work for HarCorp would make what happened at the Med Ball seem like a minor disagreement taken out of context—no one would believe the worst if he and HarCorp felt she was still the right person for the job.

Most importantly, it would give him the excuse to contact her.

He might not be able to fix the mess of his personal life, but he could solve both their business problems by simply extending an olive branch. Business he understood, and contacting Gwen would be a sound business choice with benefits to both parties.

He clicked open a new e-mail and chose his words carefully.

What happened after this…well, that would really be up to Gwen. He'd keep an open and optimistic mind.

Gwen,
HarCorp's meeting with Hiramine is still on for Friday at one. After all the prep work you put in on this project, I'm assuming you'd like to see it through to the end.

HarCorp could use your expertise in making this meeting a success, and I'd consider it a professional favor if you'd be able to put our differences aside and assist as originally planned.

Gwen watched Sarah's face as she read the printout of Will's e-mail. She drummed her fingernails on Sarah's antique dining room table in impatience as she waited. Sarah's plan for a non-Will, get-back-to-real-life dinner had been sidetracked when Gwen produced Will's e-mail. Gwen needed a sounding board for this new development, but jeez, how slow did her sister read? "Well, what do you make of it?"

Sarah flipped over the paper as if more might be on the other side then looked at her in mild shock. "This is it? No explanation? No phone call?"

"That's it. Out of nowhere into my in-box this afternoon." She sighed and pushed at the potatoes on her plate. She appreciated Sarah's efforts at dinner, but tonight Gwen had little appetite for even Sarah's fool-proof comfort food.

"Do you think it's an opening? Some kind of attempt at reconciliation?" Sarah handed the printout back across the table to Gwen.

"I don't know what to think." Gwen smoothed her fingers over the words in the paper as if the answers might be in Braille. "That's why I haven't answered yet.

"On the one hand, he all but calls me on my contractual obligations—which he's fully within his rights to do so—but last week my contract didn't seem to matter. On the other…"

Sarah nodded. "It's tough to tell *what* he's thinking."

"Try 'impossible,'" Gwen muttered, as she moved the irritating e-mail off the table and pushed at her food some more.

"I meant," Sarah continued, "it's so vague. Someone needs to explain to him the great invention of the emoticon. I can't tell if it's just business or if he's trying to apologize."

"Welcome to my world." Gwen sighed.

"Are you going to do it?"

"I don't know. I did sign a contract, but I haven't been paid yet. I'd be in violation of the contract if I don't follow through, but other than losing the check, there's not much more professional harm that could be done. What's he going to do? Not give me a reference?" She snorted before she caught herself. "It's not like one is forthcoming at this point anyway."

Sarah's level look pinned Gwen to her chair. "But you want to do it. In a purely professional sense, I mean."

Gwen felt her mouth twitch. "Yeah. Kinda. It would be nice to see it all the way through, and it would be a nice feather in my cap. Plus, it would show that regardless of anything else going on, I can still do my job."

"Unlike before?"

"I wasn't given the opportunity before. When everything hit the fan, I was out the door before any of the other projects I was working on came to fruition."

"That was your own fault. You let David—"

She didn't need Sarah harping on that again. "Yes, I know that *now*. The thing is, no one's seen what I can really do. If I make it through the next couple of weeks with my reputation intact, my success with this meeting could open more doors for me."

"And on a personal level?"

There was that headache again, softly throbbing behind her eyes. "I want to, but I don't. I love him, but I can't just put myself out there for him to hurt me again. Being in the same room with him would be a nightmare."

Sarah nodded.

"But I know how important this is for him. I don't hate him enough yet to want him to fail." She sighed, the indecision eating at her.

"You're going to do it, aren't you, Gwennie? It's a win-win situation. You'd be making a sound business decision—and it will be good for your bank account as well. You should do it because it's the right thing for *you,* not because you're in love with him."

"Oh, no. I'm not considering doing it because I love him. Quite the opposite. He accused me of using him. Now it looks like he's using me. So we'll use each other, and we'll both come out ahead."

"And if this offer is more than just business?"

Gwen shrugged. "I can't infer that it is, and I won't get my hopes up."

"Smart girl." Sarah patted her hand. "But don't completely ignore the possibility."

"I guess I've made my decision, huh?"

"Sounds like it."

"Can I borrow your laptop for a minute?"

Sarah arched an eyebrow at her. "In the middle of dinner, Miss Behavior? Aren't there rules about that?"

Gwen lifted her own eyebrow in response. "Did you invite Miss Behavior to dinner or your sister?"

Sarah waved her hand in the direction of her desk and the laptop. "On you go. But the next time my cell phone rings, I get to answer it—no matter where we are."

"Hmm." Gwen grinned and scooted her chair back. "How about I won't mention to Mother that you offered me money to write your thank-you notes last Christmas instead?"

Sarah shrank noticeably. "You win. I'll open another bottle of wine while you're gone."

But she was already mentally composing her response. It had to be just as vague and businesslike as Will's.

Evie's natural exuberance couldn't be stifled forever, and Will was happy to see she was deigning to speak to him again. While she was still a bit cool, at least tonight's dinner wasn't the silent movie it had been recently. The tentative truce with his moody charge and the polite e-mail from Gwen waiting for him this morning informing him of her attendance at tomorrow's meeting had improved his outlook immensely.

"Parkline's open house is on Monday night. You'll get to sign up for classes and meet your teachers."

"Sounds great." Evie cut her beef with precise movements. "I'll need to go next week and get my uniform."

"The entire board of trustees will be at the open house," he added casually. "That includes Mrs. Wellford."

Evie started to nod, then froze midchew. Her eyes widened, and she swallowed with difficulty. "The lady with the dog?"

I will not laugh. "Yes, the lady with the dog. Its name is Shu-Shu, and you should probably be prepared to make amends."

Evie looked horrified. "It was an accident, Will, and I know better now. Surely Mrs. Wellford won't hold a grudge."

Evie paused, and when she winced, Will knew she was picturing Shu-Shu retching on Mrs. Wellford's white, lace collar. Lord knew it wasn't a visual he'd forget anytime soon.

"Oh, no, she will, won't she? I think I hate that dog."

"You and everyone else." He chuckled. "Just be prepared."

"Gwen says it's not polite to remind someone of past errors, so Mrs. Wellford would be rude to bring it up. But I'll apologize again anyway. Gwen said it couldn't hurt."

The mention of Gwen had him wondering if he should tell Evie about tomorrow. She'd be pleased, of course, and his making peace with Gwen would go a long way in warming her attitude, but he didn't want her jumping to any assumptions about Gwen being a part of his—or their—future.

"Just so you know, Gwen has agreed to help with my meeting tomorrow."

Evie's facade cracked, bringing the ear-to-ear grin he'd missed recently. "Really? So you two made up? Did you apologize? Is she—?"

"Evie, don't jump ahead. This is strictly business. Gwen has an expertise I need for this meeting, and we're simply sticking to the terms of her contract."

Evie's face fell. "Will, don't be a butthead about this."

"Evangeline, if you call me a butthead one more time, you'll be an old woman before you see the inside of a dressing room at Neiman Marcus again."

Evie closed her mouth with an audible snap. *Finally a threat with enough teeth.* He'd have to remember that one.

"Sorry. I just mean it's great that you've decided to work with Gwen on this. I know her pretty well, and I know she's going to do a great job for you. But—" she paused to lay her fork and knife down carefully before she leveled a look at him that was mature beyond her years "—I also know you pretty well now, too. If you keep acting like a butt—I mean, acting like this, you'll drive her away and she'll never come back."

"I know you miss Gwen and you were hoping she might be a permanent addition to the family, but this isn't about you, Evie."

"Oh, I know that. But I know Gwen cares about you—I think she might even love you. This is your chance to show Gwen how much you care about her. You do care about her, right?"

Evie's insight shocked him. As much as he wanted to steer her to a different, less uncomfortable, subject, he felt this conversation might be an important turning point in his relationship with Evie.

"I do care about her. And I know you'll be happy to hear I've realized that I may have been a bit hasty in my judgment of her. My only defense for my actions is wanting to protect you—and me, too. There are plenty of people out there who are only looking out for themselves."

Evie grinned at his revelation. "I know. But Gwen isn't one of them."

He returned the grin. "Hopefully not."

"So you'll apologize?"

"Yep." *As soon as the meeting is over and only if she seems to be open to it.*

"And you'll ask her to move back in with us?"

"Whoa, slow down there."

"But, Will—"

"We'll see how it goes."

Gwen dressed carefully Friday morning. Knee-length navy-blue skirt, light blue silk shirt, closed-toe pumps and understated jewelry. She started to twist her hair up into a French knot, but with the overly conservative outfit, it only made her look like a spinster librarian.

Normally that look would be considered fine for a meeting, but Will's presence at *this* meeting changed everything. She shook her hair out and let it fall in loose waves around her shoulders. Will liked her hair better this way, but the Japanese guests would find it odd. She compromised by clipping it at the base of her neck.

Gwen packed her briefcase and glanced at her watch. She'd meet with Nancy first to go over all the small details one last time. Then she'd meet with Will and his VPs for one last briefing before Mr. Hiramine and his group arrived.

She took a deep breath and checked her lipstick one last time. An eerie sense of déjà vu settled on her shoulders. The last time she darkened HarCorp's doors, she'd been so excited and positive her meeting with Will would change her life.

How right she'd been. It had almost destroyed her.

She should have the same feeling today—and she did. Sort of. The feeling this meeting could change everything was there, only this time she lacked the excitement and hopeful expectations.

Unlike last time, at least she knew—somewhat—what she was getting into.

This time, she knew to guard her heart.

CHAPTER FIFTEEN

"WHERE the hell is Gwen?" Will paced his office and glanced at the clock again. Twenty minutes until show time, and Gwen was nowhere to be found.

Nancy bustled in carrying his suit jacket. "She's in the boardroom, briefing the others. You're late."

Will shrugged into the jacket and adjusted his tie. "Then let's go."

HarCorp's executive conference room took up the entire top corner of the building, and through the glass walls, Will could see his VPs lined up like school kids as Gwen lectured animatedly in front of them. Nancy opened the main door and he could hear her going over last-minute reminders.

"Remember—no big hand gestures while you talk. They won't call you by your first name, so don't ask. And remember to use 'Mr.'—this isn't the time to create false familiarity by just calling them by just their last names. All right?"

Silent nods answered her. Will could relate. When Gwen was in Miss Behavior mode, a man couldn't do much more. She simply projected an aura that made people want to be on their very best behavior. As several men noticed him and nodded, Gwen turned to see who was behind her.

One brief flicker in those hazel eyes of hers gave him a flash of hope that this meeting might be good for something other than HarCorp's profits. A split-second later, the look was gone, and her mouth curved into a noncommittal smile. "Good afternoon, Mr. Harrison. We're just going over a few last-minute things."

Her cool greeting irritated him, but he shook it off with a sharp mental reminder: *This is business. What did you expect? A big kiss?*

He inclined his head slightly. "Miss Sawyer."

Gwen indicated a chair at the table. "You'll sit here, Mr. Harrison. Mr. Hiramine and Mr. Takeshi will be over here."

He watched as she arranged people and water glasses to her satisfaction. He could tell she was tense as she looked everything over with a critical eye, but the rest of the occupants of the room would never be able to tell. Matthews from Marketing tried to pull him into conversation, and he answered absently.

His eyes feasted on her, forcefully reminding him how empty his bed had felt recently. As she laughed at something Andrews said to her, he felt a stab of jealousy in his heart. More than anything, he wanted to drag her to his office, tell her he forgave her and spend the next couple of hours showing her exactly how much he missed her.

But he had to make it through this meeting first. As he watched, Gwen demonstrated to his VP of Accounting how to bow, and he knew he'd been right to hire her in the first place. Even in some awful old-lady outfit complete with sensible shoes, she radiated poise and confidence.

The weight of the meeting lifted off his shoulders. With Gwen in charge, he had no doubt of the outcome. Just the sight of her filled him with surety of that fact. Gwen knew her stuff and had everyone and everything firmly in hand. Thank God he decided to use her for this.

Out of nowhere, his own words came back to him. *She was using us.* Guilt filled him. Was he any better? Was this any different? He was using her right now, after all.

Realization hit him like lightning. Utilizing someone's

talents wasn't the same as using the person. Gwen's defense—
I lobbied HarCorp. I never lobbied you—made a lot more
sense now. She may have been using the situation to her advantage, but she wasn't necessarily using him. And taking advantage of the situation wasn't a bad thing, either. If it was,
he was just as guilty.

And with that realization, he could now admit Gwen was
more than just under his skin without sounding like a gullible fool. Somehow, in the middle of all of this, he'd fallen
in love with her.

He was out of his seat, fully intending to march Gwen out
of the conference room for a private meeting of their own when
she suddenly straightened and clapped her hands for everyone's
attention. With a small inclination of her head toward the
hallway, she brought him back to the situation at hand.

"It's showtime, gentlemen. Here they come."

Three years of work was about to be decided, and suddenly,
Will couldn't care less.

Gwen knew the meeting went well. No major gaffes to offend
the Japanese guests, and HarCorp's VPs kept their usual
aggressive American business tactics to themselves. Mr.
Hiramine's assistant, Mr. Takeshi, served as translator when
needed, freeing Gwen to help steer the meeting properly. She
couldn't have been more pleased.

But her stomach was still tied in knots, and had been since
Will walked into the room and caused every nerve cell in her
body to cry out to him. The long, level looks he kept sending
in her direction were unreadable, and the uncertainty they
caused made her slightly nauseous.

Her position at his left side kept her senses on overload
during the meeting, and her focus shifted too often from the
business going on around her to the smell of his aftershave
and the sight of that place on his neck right above his collar
where he liked to be kissed. Her ability to concentrate evapo-

rated each time his arm brushed against hers or his leg bumped hers under the massive table. She had to call on every ounce of her pride, her professionalism and her training to keep the smile on her face and her head in the general vicinity of the game.

And then it was over. There was much bowing and shaking of hands, then the line of men in dark suits filed from the room. Will followed as far as the door and shut it behind them. With the meeting behind her and a safe distance between them, Gwen was able to draw a deep breath for the first time in hours. As she exhaled, she realized she'd made one last error.

"You should escort them as far as the elevator, Will," she whispered, moving in the direction of the door.

"They'll survive." Will perched a hip on the conference table. "So how do you think it went?"

"Good. Really good."

"You don't think they sounded unenthused about the idea?"

"That's normal. I warned you the Japanese could seem very reserved and formal. It doesn't mean they aren't interested in proceeding. It could mean quite the opposite. My feeling is that you'll hear good news soon." She tried for a bright smile, but it felt fake.

Will nodded, but didn't say anything. The silence, combined with that same stare he'd given her throughout the meeting, tightened the knot in her stomach even more.

"Thank you for your help. It wouldn't have gone as well without your input. I appreciate it."

"You're welcome."

The stilted, polite conversation was killing her. As soon as she could get out of here, she was getting a strong drink.

Will fished in his pocket and pulled out a piece of paper. "Here's your check." He slid it across the table to her.

As awkward as it was, she had no choice but to take it. "Thank you. You could've just had Nancy mail it. I—" She lost her train of thought when she caught sight of the numbers.

That was more than her contract outlined. Like twenty percent more. She looked at Will in question.

"You did a great job, Gwen, especially considering the, uh, history we have."

Anger bubbled up inside her chest. It was a nice change from the nausea.

"HarCorp has always believed in rewarding good service from its employees. Consider it a bonus."

He sat there calling her just another employee while in the same breath he brought up their history? Anger continued to surge through her veins, warming her skin. She'd like to shove his "bonus" up his...

"Excuse me?" Will was the picture of shock.

Too late, she realized she'd vocalized the thought. *Oh God.* Her first instinct was to backtrack, but the anger fueled her forward instead.

"You heard me. I don't want your bonus." She ripped the check into small pieces, gaining great satisfaction from the look on his face. "You've embarrassed me publicly and insulted me personally, and you try to smooth it all over with a fat check?" She sneered the words. "Good God, you think you can just throw money at people to solve your problems. Grow up."

"I don't—"

"Yes, you do. First Evie, and now me." She was shouting, but she didn't care. God, it felt good to vent. She gathered up the last of her things and shoved them in her bag. "I'm not a whore, so there's no need to pay me for the sex, and if you're trying to salve your own conscience for some reason, it's really not necessary. Have Nancy mail me a check for the correct amount. I've fulfilled my end of my contract—both contracts, actually—and since I don't work for you anymore, I can now tell you what a first-class jerk you are." She looked at him levelly. "I don't want your bonus money."

The phone on the conference room table beeped. To her surprise, Will ignored it.

"I'm not paying you for sex." His mouth quirked upward. "I don't have *that* much money, you know."

Was that some kind of compliment? And what the hell did he find so funny?

"But maybe I was trying to salve my conscience." He slid off the table and walked toward her. "I know I cost you some business with my behavior. I was simply trying to offset the effects."

The phone on the table beeped again. Gwen glanced at it and noticed the red intercom light flashing. Probably Nancy. Will continued as if he hadn't heard it.

"I wasn't trying to insult you further."

He was close—too close for Gwen's comfort—and she forgot about the beeping phone as, once again, Will's presence managed to shrink her perception to just the two of them. The fire behind her anger cooled some, leaving her confused at her jumbled thoughts and emotions.

That half smile appeared again. "You know, I don't think I've ever heard you shout like that. Miss Behavior wouldn't approve."

As she calmed, the belated embarrassment at losing her temper crept in. Quietly, and surprised she had the guts to vocalize the thought, she whispered, "Well, you didn't hurt Miss Behavior. You hurt me."

"I know. And I'm sorry." He stepped closer and her breath caught.

The damn BlackBerry in Will's pocket chirped.

Will's eyes never left hers. "Gwen?"

It chirped again, the sound—and Will's lack of reaction—grating on her last nerve. When Will didn't move, she snapped. "Aren't you going to answer that? Nancy's probably—"

He shook his head. "It'll wait. This is more important."

What? "Huh?"

"'Flesh and blood people always take priority over any other message in any other medium.'"

Her shock must have shown on her face, because he laughed.

"I've been paying attention. And you are certainly my priority right now." His hand reached out to stroke the side of her face. The sensation, coupled with his quiet words, rocked her. "I miss you. I'd like the chance to start over, if you're willing to give it to me."

Her chest ached.

"You've civilized me and domesticated me. I'd like for you to love me."

The last bit of hurt pride propping up her defenses crumbled, and a happy, hopeful bubble inflated in her chest. "I do."

Will's face lit up. "Really?"

She could feel a big goofy grin pulling at her cheeks. "Yeah."

And then Will was kissing her, and every feeling she'd been trying to bury exploded back to the forefront. Her body sighed into his, and a feeling of *rightness* flooded her. His kiss turned hungry, and she responded, ignoring the strange knocking sound...

"Mr. Harrison!"

She broke away and saw Nancy standing in the now-open door, her fist frozen in midknock. Horror flooded through her as she saw Mr. Hiramine and his entourage standing behind Nancy. Oh God. They'd seen her crawling all over Will...

Will didn't even have the good grace to look embarrassed. Of course, her face was hot enough for both of them.

"Yes, Nancy, is there a problem?"

Gwen tried to step away from Will, but his hand on her arm stopped him. Short of looking like a fool trying to wiggle out of his grasp, she had no choice but to continue to stand there.

"You didn't answer my calls." Nancy was the picture of shock, but Gwen couldn't tell if it was from the scene she walked in on or Will ignoring his BlackBerry.

"I was busy."

"I see that now. But Mr. Takeshi wanted to speak with you."

Gwen stepped forward as far as Will's arm would allow. "I apologize for the, um, scene you witnessed. Mr. Harrison and I—"

"Please do not apologize, Miss Sawyer." Mr. Takeshi's young face was kind and slightly amused. "Mr. Hiramine was aware that you and Mr. Harrison had some kind of unfinished business and we are sorry to have interrupted your…reconciliation, should we say?"

Mr. Hiramine leaned in and said something in rapid Japanese, of which Gwen only caught a few words.

His assistant translated. "Mr. Hiramine says he looks forward to doing additional business with HarCorp, but we leave you now to settle your own matters. We will be in touch." With a shallow bow, he turned and led his group back in the direction of the elevator.

Nancy mouthed "I'm sorry" as she closed the door behind them.

Gwen sunk into a chair, her knees weak at the thought of how that scene could have easily undermined all of her hard work. She was just destined, it seemed, to be caught in compromising positions. "Well, that was embarrassing."

Will shrugged as he kneeled in front of her chair. His hands caressed her knees, sending shivers up her spine. "You care too much what others think."

She might as well get everything out in the open. "You know what happened in D.C."

He nodded. "Yeah. It wasn't all your fault, though. And I think you could have repaired the damage if you hadn't left town so quickly."

Sarah had said the same thing dozens of times, but for some reason hearing it from Will made her believe it.

"But it was a good thing you did leave."

She felt her jaw drop. "What?"

Will just laughed at her. "Because you wouldn't be here

otherwise, and I wouldn't have a major business deal to celebrate."

Realization dawned. "What am I thinking? I should be congratulating you on sealing the deal."

Will's smile caused her heart to skip a beat. "With you in charge, was there ever a doubt?"

"You're just lucky we didn't lose it all right there at the end. I think we broke about forty-seven rules of etiquette with that display."

He stood and took hold of her hands. "Again, you worry too much, Miss Behavior. In fact, there's only one etiquette rule I care about right now."

"And that would be?"

"The one about 'flesh and blood' being the most important thing." Will pulled her out of the chair and into his arms.

With her body molded to his, she had no problem feeling *his* flesh and blood pressing insistently against her.

She giggled. "If you want to use the phone…"

"You're hysterical." Will's lips caught hers in a tender kiss, full of promise.

"Check your BlackBerry?"

"The only thing I need to check is whether the door is locked this time." With a groan, he lifted Gwen by the hips and settled her on the table. Standing between her legs, he moved in for a long, leisurely nuzzle down the sensitive skin of her neck.

Gwen put on her primmest, most proper Miss Behavior tone. "Sex on the conference room table during office hours is hardly proper etiquette. I thought you said you were civilized now."

Will didn't pause, and Gwen tipped her head back to give him better access. "Well, maybe it's time to redefine 'civilized behavior.' Some of your etiquette rules seem pretty old-fashioned. You should make new ones."

Her usual argument died in her throat as Will nibbled the

magic spot beneath her ear. For once, Miss Behavior totally agreed with him.

"You know what? Forget the rules."

* * * * *

Turn the page for an exclusive extract from
RAFFAELE: TAMING HIS TEMPESTUOUS VIRGIN
by
Sandra Marton

"In that case," Don Cordiano said, "I give my daughter's hand to my faithful second in command, Antonio Giglio."

At last, the woman's head came up. "No," she whispered. "No," she said again, and the cry grew, gained strength, until she was shrieking it. "No! No! No!"

Rafe stared at her. No wonder she'd sounded familiar. Those wide, violet eyes. The small, straight nose. The sculpted cheekbones, the lush, rosy mouth...

"Wait a minute," Rafe said, "just wait one damned minute...."

Chiara swung toward him. The American knew. Not that it mattered. She was trapped. Trapped! Giglio was an enormous blob of flesh; he had wet-looking red lips and his face was always sweaty. But it was his eyes that made her shudder, and he had taken to watching her with a boldness that was terrifying. She had to do something....

Desperate, she wrenched her hand from her father's.

"I will tell you the truth, Papa. You cannot give me to Giglio. You see—you see, the American and I have already met."

"You're damned right we have," Rafe said furiously. "On the road coming here. Your daughter stepped out of the trees and—"

"I only meant to greet him. As a gesture of—of goodwill." She swallowed hard. Her eyes met Rafe's and a long-forgotten memory swept through him: being caught in a firefight in some miserable hellhole of a country when a terrified cat, eyes wild with fear, had suddenly, inexplicably run into the middle of it. "But—but he—he took advantage."

Rafe strode toward her. "Try telling your old man what really happened!"

"What *really* happened," she said in a shaky whisper, "is that…is that right there, in his car—right there, Papa, Signor Orsini tried to seduce me!"

Giglio cursed. Don Cordiano roared. Rafe would have said, "You're crazy, all of you," but Chiara Cordiano's dark lashes fluttered and she fainted, straight into his arms.

* * * * *

Be sure to look for
RAFFAELE: TAMING HIS TEMPESTUOUS VIRGIN
by Sandra Marton
available November 2009 from Harlequin Presents®!

HARLEQUIN *Presents*

TWO CROWNS, TWO ISLANDS, ONE LEGACY

A royal family torn apart by pride and its lust for power, reunited by purity and passion

THE ROYAL HOUSE *of* KAREDES

Look for the next passionate adventure in
The Royal House of Karedes:

THE GREEK BILLIONAIRE'S INNOCENT PRINCESS
by Chantelle Shaw, November 2009

THE FUTURE KING'S LOVE-CHILD
by Melanie Milburne, December 2009

RUTHLESS BOSS, ROYAL MISTRESS
by Natalie Anderson, January 2010

THE DESERT KING'S HOUSEKEEPER BRIDE
by Carol Marinelli, February 2010

HP12867

*She's his mistress on demand—but when
he wants her body and soul, he will be
demanding a whole lot more!
Dare we say it…even marriage!*

PLAYBOY BOSS, LIVE-IN MISTRESS
by *Kelly Hunter*

Playboy Alexander always gets what he wants…
and he wants his personal assistant Sienna as his
mistress! Forced into close confinement, Sienna
realizes Alex isn't a man to take no for an answer.…

Book #2873

Available November 2009

Look for more of these hot stories throughout the year
from Harlequin Presents!

EXTRA

SNOW, SATIN AND SEDUCTION

Unwrapped by the Billionaire!

It's nearly Christmas and four billionaires are looking for the perfect gift to unwrap—a virgin perhaps, or a convenient wife?

One thing's for sure, when the snow is falling outside, these billionaires will be keeping warm inside, between their satin sheets.

Collect all of these wonderful festive titles in November from the Presents EXTRA line!

The Millionaire's Christmas Wife #77
by HELEN BROOKS

The Christmas Love-Child #78
by JENNIE LUCAS

Royal Baby, Forbidden Marriage #79
by KATE HEWITT

Bedded at the Billionaire's Convenience #80
by CATHY WILLIAMS

You're invited to join our Tell Harlequin Reader Panel!

By joining our new reader panel you will:

- Receive Harlequin® books—they are FREE and yours to keep with no obligation to purchase anything!
- Participate in fun online surveys
- Exchange opinions and ideas with women just like you
- Have a say in our new book ideas and help us publish the best in women's fiction

In addition, you will have a chance to win great prizes and receive special gifts!
See Web site for details. Some conditions apply.
Space is limited.

To join, visit us at
www.TellHarlequin.com.

REQUEST YOUR FREE BOOKS!

HARLEQUIN *Presents*®

2 FREE NOVELS
PLUS 2
FREE GIFTS!

PASSION GUARANTEED SEDUCTION

I ♥

HARLEQUIN® *Presents*

BROUGHT TO YOU BY FANS OF
HARLEQUIN PRESENTS.

We are its editors and authors
and biggest fans—and we'd
love to hear from YOU!

Subscribe today to our online blog at
www.iheartpresents.com